THE UNEASY SUN

The Uneasy Sun

Michael Butterworth

ISBN: 979-8-3372-0435-2

This edition published in 2026 by Open Road Integrated Media, Inc.
180 Maiden Lane
New York, NY 10038
www.openroadmedia.com

For all my friends on St. Paul's gentle islands

THE UNEASY SUN

CHAPTER 1

Deborah Tarrant came to the islands on a Tuesday night in September. She came in a planeload of holidaymaking British and homeward-turning Maltese; over the wrinkled, pale crest of Mont Blanc and down the length of the Italian coast, where sheet lightning played on inland hills.

A handsome lad in a striped shirt rescued her from the jostling crush in the airport lounge, calling out her name till she heard him and waved back over the bobbing heads. He took her cases and led her out to his waiting taxi.

It was half an hour's drive through a dark countryside of low hills and dry stone walls overhung with prickly pear, where cicadas shrilled; through the streets of stately towns, long and lit-up, with people strolling—children even—though it was four o'clock in the morning. Once the road dipped under an escarpment, and she saw a Baroque mass above her, floodlit lime green and gold to resemble a stupendous birthday cake, and the boy told her this was Mdina—the Citta Notabile, the notable city.

The hotel came all unexpectedly out of the darkness like a white ship, and she could hear the sound of waves on shingle somewhere far below. Another smiling, dark face—and a shirt-sleeved giant took her cases and led her across the tiled floor of a deserted foyer. There was a child's bucket and spade lying forlornly by the door of the lift.

When her guide snapped on the lights of Room 28, she saw a green-tiled floor, fitted cupboards, a dressing table, long curtains hanging limply by an open French window—and *two* single beds. And the shock of it nearly made her cry out.

Then: 'I asked them to change the booking to a single room!'

He shook his head and smiled.

'A single room. I particularly asked for a single room!' Oh, God, she thought. He doesn't speak any English.

His big hand went to a bulging hip pocket and brought out a folded slip of paper.

'Mees Tarrant,' he said complacently. 'Room twenny-eight. Is okay.' And his amiable peasant's face creased in a lovely smile.

'All right,' said Deborah helplessly. 'I'll see them at the reception desk in the morning and get it changed.'

'Mees?'

'I said it will be all right for the rest of the night,' she cried. 'There's no need for you to bother. I'll see them tomorrow . . .'

'Tomorrow?'

'Don't worry.' She fumbled in her handbag and thrust half a crown into the huge palm. 'Good night. And thank you.'

He nodded vigorously, backing to the door.

'Good night, mees. I hope you have very happy stay in Malta.' It was obviously his set-piece. 'Very nice hotel, very nice room. Yes?'

'Yes,' said Deborah faintly.

Alone, she looked at her watch. Four-thirty. She hadn't slept during the flight, thanks to her private terror of airplanes, and she was dog-tired. Nothing else but to make the best of it; her mind baulked at the notion of sitting till morning in the downstairs foyer, under the hurt gaze of the big night porter.

She dared herself to look at the second bed: the alien one nearest the window. It was a grim reminder she certainly hadn't bargained for. How could they have done it to her?

Later—when she lay down and resigned herself to the warm half-darkness—she kept her face turned to the wall, so that she should not see the other bed, for fear of what might appear there in the dead wasteland between wakefulness and oblivion.

The gentle ruffling of the curtains woke her, and she sat up with the Mediterranean sunlight streaming in, and across the empty bed next to hers.

Crossing to the window, barefoot on the warm tiles, she looked out upon the shimmering blueness of a bay far below; to a white-sanded beach, where a half-naked boy was laying out deckchairs; to the far headland, where an ancient stone tower stood sentinel over the deathly stillness of the morning sky and sea.

'It's going to be all right,' she said aloud. 'I can put all the past behind me. The future begins here . . . now.'

Suddenly alive, she showered in the private bathroom, and put on her "bold face", which meant lots of pale lipstick, with her hair brushed back casually under a linen band.

She examined herself critically in the dressing table mirror: psychedelic-print pyjama suit over a matching bikini.

'I certainly don't *look* haunted,' she told herself. 'Not haunted enough, that is, to frighten away every eligible male in sight—I hope!' And she laughed.

Placing her cases firmly outside in the corridor, she slammed the door of Room 28 and walked down towards the lift. As she did so, there was a mixed babble of voices, a door opened, and a family of five poured out into her path. The parents' sun-reddened faces were turned to her briefly and without interest, then went back to their riotous offspring.

'Mind where you're walking, Fiona . . . don't shove so, Gary!'

'How sweet,' murmured Deborah, touching a small, flaxen head. 'Good morning, all.'

No one replied. They went on their way down the curving staircase, and Deborah remained by the lift, feeling unaccountably flattened by the encounter. The bright smile she summoned up to greet the opening doors of the lift was met by a set of red—and it seemed to her—angry faces, but there was a small, dark-haired boy—his bowed head barely reaching to her waist—who murmured to himself in a grave and singsong voice while he plucked the petals from a hibiscus flower and strewed them on the floor.

'One for sorrow,
Two for mirth
Three for a wedding,
Four for a birth . . .'

Then they were down in the foyer, and it was all quite different from the way it had been pre-dawn: a crowded kaleidoscope of brown limbs and holiday casuals. Deborah stood and watched the boy wander slowly in the wake of an auburn-haired girl towards the glass doors of the restaurant, still muttering his incantation. When he was out of sight, she turned towards the reception desk, where a man in a floral-patterned shirt was coping with all comers:

'Conducted tour of Mdina and Rabat, including the Catacombs, Roman Villa and the Maltese lace industries, madame. Bus leaves at nine-thirty . . . the bus to Valletta leaves every hour on the half-hour, sir . . . Postcards for the U.K.? Threepence, sir. Yes, madame?' . . . world-weary, dark eyes lighted on Deborah and swam down her figure appraisingly.

'Ahm . . . about my room . . .' she faltered.

'You arrived last night, miss? . . .'

'Tarrant.'

His eyes swivelled to the key rack. 'Room twenty-eight,' he said, puzzled. 'The room's all right, isn't it?'

She felt her lower lip begin to tremble. It was appalling to have to spell out the hideous thing to this man in public; there were more people forming up at the counter; a big woman at her elbow was breathing heavily with impatience.

'I . . . I wrote to you,' she said, by way of prompting him; and when this drew no reaction: 'to change the original reservation from a double to a single room.'

'There were to have been two persons?' he asked.

'Yes,' she whispered. The big woman seemed to quell her impatience. She was probably all ears now. God knows what she was thinking . . .

He crossed over to the desk behind the counter, where a young girl was writing in a ledger, and muttered to her in Maltese. The girl looked sharply at Deborah, and took up a box file, riffling through a sheaf of correspondence. Moments later, she gave a start and whispered something which made him smack his forehead.

He came back to the counter, and the girl's eyes were pansy-soft with compassion as she smiled shyly across at Deborah.

'Miss Tarrant, I am most terribly sorry,' he said. 'I remember now. We received your letter, of course, and the adjustment was made. You will have Room sixteen—a single room—from midday today. Unfortunately it's occupied till then, and this is why we had to accommodate you in twenty-eight last night.'

'I see,' said Deborah, relieved. 'Thank you.'

'We were most sorry to hear of your bereavement, Miss Tarrant,' he said earnestly. 'I hope that . . . nevertheless . . . you will enjoy a pleasant . . .' his eyes wavered with embarrassment. Deborah was already walking away towards the restaurant, conscious of all the curious, regarding eyes.

All down the long room, between the crowded tables, she felt the eyes upon her, and it seemed that the shrill chattering stopped at her passing, and then resumed, as if she carried with her a zone of breathless silence. She walked with her gaze fixed on the face of a waiter at the far end, and it was he who beckoned her to a table for one, and drew back the chair for her.

With the heartwarming Maltese smile, he handed her a menu. Deborah asked for orange juice and coffee. And then she steeled her nerve to look up.

No one was taking the slightest notice of her.

She was lying face-downwards near the water's edge, with the spent wavelets dribbling away the soft sand beneath her toes. Somewhere to her right, in the front row of deckchairs, a middle-aged north country couple were arguing in the flat, disinterested tones of lifelong acrimony. There was the pounding of children's running feet in the sand, and more children shrieking and splashing out in the shallows; cicadas had begun a chattering chorus from the gaunt cliffs all round.

The beach was filling up, yet she had never known such a feeling of separateness. It was as if she were lying on a dead sea shore of a dying moon. Surely, if she opened her eyes again, there would be no one to see her behind the dark glasses. Cautiously, she opened them, and squinted secretly along the shore line.

He was still there. Sitting cross-legged on an upturned boat at the end of the beach, under the cliff; talking and gesticulating forcefully to a pair of husky Maltese beach boys. Near-naked like them, his splendidly formed body was only marginally lighter in tone than theirs, yet his plastered-down hair was sun-bleached to whiteness, and she had already decided that his eyes were surely cornflower blue.

(Oh, girl! Be your age. Don't start weaving a fantasy around that beautiful hunk of beefcake. Why, he's probably got "philanderer" marked on his birth certificate. You'd run screaming if he so much as spoke to you . . .)

They were laughing together now at some lively remark from the blond Adonis: white-toothed, thick-throated, male-sounding laughter, rising above all the other sounds of the beach. Then he was grinning about him, winning glances. His eyes panned towards Deborah-shifted—and moved back.

(He's spotted me, and he's going to come over!)

She shut her eyes tightly and pressed her cheek against the sand. Elbows against her sides, she hugged her bra closer to her, and waited for the sound of his barefoot approach.

(This is ridiculous. Ridiculous. I don't even *like* men who look like that!)

Nothing happened. And when she looked again, the group had been joined by an auburn-haired girl in a bikini and the small boy whom Deborah recognised as the one she'd seen in the lift. Adonis was holding the lad's skinny little form high in his hands, and he was kicking and yelling to be let down; the girl stood in a self-conscious model-girl's-type pose, inclining her head so that a side curl could fall and caress her cheek. Moments later, they were all running into the sea together, whooping and laughing; the girl and Adonis were hand-in-hand.

Deborah smiled to herself, and rolled over on her back. Curiously contented, she yielded to the heat and to the langorous, small sounds of the sea. And soon she was asleep . . .

'Hello.' A young voice, shyly ingratiating.

Deborah sat up, and rescued her bra straps. It was the small boy. He was looking down at her, and scooping fine featherings of sand with the toe of one skinny foot.

'Hello there,' she smiled. 'Did you enjoy your swim?'

Without replying, he sat down close to her with his thin arms wrapped round his legs, and his chin resting on his knees, staring gravely out to sea. The drying salt water had traced rivulets of whiteness on his dark skin.

'What a beautiful tan,' said Deborah. 'You must have been here quite a while.' And when he didn't answer: I usually tan quite painlessly, but I know I shall suffer this evening for falling asleep in the sun on my first day.'

Then, with a sudden stab of pity, she saw that he was crying. Not in an obvious way; but when he blinked, his eyelids expressed a fresh tear on to his peach-downed cheek. Deborah had had no experience of small boys' emotional problems, but she knew instinctively that—though she was probably supposed to notice, indeed the tears were almost certainly displayed for her benefit—she mustn't comment directly. She racked her brain for an oblique approach, but he forstalled her:

'I hate Danny!' he growled. 'He's always picking on me. Lots of people pick on me, but he does it nearly all the time. Rotten bully. I hope he dies.'

'Who's Danny?' she asked. 'The big man with fair hair?'

'I wish I could die too,' he said. 'It isn't a bad thing being dead. Lot better being dead than stuck on this beastly beach all the time. And she won't take me to see the armour.' He turned to regard Deborah, and the tears seemed to have checked. 'You didn't have any breakfast this morning,' he said. 'Only coffee and fruit juice. We were sitting behind you, and I watched. Why weren't you hungry?'

She laughed: 'I don't often eat breakfast; what's more, I

arrived here in the early hours of this morning, and I was much too tired to have an appetite.'

The dark eyes looked her over dispassionately. 'Well, you're quite fat,' he said, 'for someone who never eats breakfast.'

'Thank you, kind sir,' she said, amused.

'I didn't mean to be rude,' he said gravely. 'I think you're just nice, actually. Gloria's much too fat. Bulgy.' He grimaced.

'Who's Gloria?'

'She's my nanny. The one with the red hair. We're on holiday together, only she never takes me anywhere. She only wants to be on the beach . . .' he glanced over his shoulder, then leaned forward conspiratorially '. . . Gloria's in love with Danny. Know how I know?'

Deborah shook her head.

'I saw them *kissing*!' he whispered. 'They kiss quite a lot. He takes her out in his motor boat. She pretends to go for the ride, but I know. They go round the point to the other bay where there's no one to see them. And then they *kiss*!'

Having deposited this confidence in Deborah's lap, he went back to his squatting posture, and stared out to sea again.

After a while he said: 'Do you know my name?'

She shook her head.

'My name's Alec. Alec Hugo Rattigan. I know yours is Miss Tarrant because I asked at the desk. Why haven't you got a husband—you're quite old, aren't you?'

'Much too old,' she said.

'I expect you'll find someone to marry you,' he said comfortingly. 'I expect that's why you came to Malta on your own—to find a man to get married to. Do you like iced lollies?'

Deborah took the hint, and rummaged in her bag for some change to give him. She watched his small figure zigzagging through the lines of deckchairs towards the kiosk at the back of the beach, and then she lay back again with her arms behind her head.

'I'm back!' It was Alec, and he was not alone. 'Joey said you'd rather have a coffee than a lolly, so he's brought you one. This is Joey.'

Joey was obviously the boy who ran the refreshment kiosk. He wore white shorts and baseball cap. Scarcely more than a child, but a man already, with a man's confidence in his charm and handsomeness. He stooped and laid the tray beside Deborah, smiling to show his white teeth. Deborah caught the tang of shaving lotion in her nostrils, though his tanned cheek was covered in virgin down. She thanked him, and he left her with a hot-eyed glance.

'He's a bit stuck on you,' mumbled Alec, through a mouthful of melting pink ice. 'He saw you coming down to the beach, and he asked me if you had a boyfriend, or if you were alone.'

'So you told him I was looking for a husband?' smiled Deborah.

Alec's eyes were reproachful. 'Of course I didn't,' he said. 'What do you take me for? He's miles too young for you. He lives with his mother in Mgarr.'

'I'm sorry I teased you, Alec,' she said. 'But I must put you right on this. I didn't actually come to Malta to find someone to marry me. I'm only—incidentally—on my own.' Suddenly, before his innocent, regarding eyes, it became easy to say—and a relief to say it: 'I was to have come with my mother, but she was—she died last month.'

'I know quite a lot about dead people,' he said gravely. 'What did your mother die of?'

Before she could frame a reply, their attention was snatched by the sound of a high-powered engine. The blond Adonis was slicing away from the shallows in a blue speedboat with the words: DANNY'S SKI-SCHOOL lettered along its sleek hull. The red-headed Gloria rose like Venus Anodyamene from the water behind the speedboat on a single ski, and her hair trailed like a flame.

'That's all she's interested in,' growled the boy. 'Water skiing and kissing Danny. I keep asking her to take me to see the armour, but she won't.'

'What armour's this, Alec?'

The knights' armour in Valletta,' he said. 'There's a big room full of it. Helmets and swords. More helmets and swords than there is in the whole world. A boy who used to play with me—he went home last week—he went there, and he told me all about it.'

Deborah looked about her. The north country couple were sleeping on their eternal argument. The beach was now crowded; each group a part to itself—and she alone, like the garrulous, appealing little boy by her side.

She heard herself saying: 'Would you like me to take you to see the armour, Alec?'

His delight was heartwarming, and she was thankful for the impulse. 'That is, if Gloria will give her permission,' she added.

'Oh, *she* won't mind,' he said. '*She'll* be glad to get rid of me. Can we go this afternoon?'

'Yes. Why not?'

'Good. This afternoon, then. We can have an early lunch and catch the half-past one bus to Valletta. I'm glad you came, Miss Tarrant.'

'I'm glad, too, Alec.'

He seemed to be wrestling with a decision. Frowning, he scooped up a handful of damp sand and threw it forcefully at the hissing surf.

'I'd better tell you my secret,' he said at length.

'That would be nice,' she said. 'But don't if you think you'll regret it later.'

'It's my dead body,' he said unconcernedly. 'You know I told you I knew quite a lot about dead people? Well, it's because I've got a dead person of my own.'

She stared at the earnest, small face, and felt her indulgent smile wither at the edges. 'Whatever do you mean, Alec?'

'A dead person,' he said. 'I found a dead body, and no one else knows where it is but me. That's my secret.' He leaned forward and added with intensity: 'It's all wrong what they say in books, you know . . . *they don't smell at all*!'

CHAPTER 2

They stood amongst the slippery rocks at the end of the beach when the speedboat wallowed to a halt, and the girl at the end of the tow line threw up her hands with a gay laugh and sank down on her ski in the shallows. Alec splashed out to meet her, scowling at Danny when the big man vaulted out of the boat and tousled his hair roughly. Deborah waited, and watched him return with Gloria, carrying her ski over his shoulder. The auburn-haired girl's full figure moved voluptuously as she waded. Her gaze flickered to Deborah when Alec pointed.

'*That's* Miss Tarrant. She's going to take me this afternoon, only she said I had to ask you first. But it's all right, isn't it?'

At close quarters, the girl's skin was muddy under her heavy tan, and her green eyes were marginally hostile; they peered myopically, like the eyes of someone who should have been wearing glasses, but probably didn't through conceit.

'You can if you like, but I can tell you you'll find him a bit of a handful.' Her accent was Americanised Cockney. While she spoke, she was pricing Deborah's bikini.

'We already get on quite famously,' said Deborah. 'I'm

fortunate in not having much experience of six-year-old boys, and it all comes as an amusing surprise.'

This remark won a blank stare of incomprehension, and then the girl switched to Danny, who was dragging the speedboat on to the beach with a great display of rippling back-muscles.

'I can go to Comino with you after all,' she called. 'This woman's taking him out this afternoon.'

'How very agreeable,' said Danny, dissociating himself from the girl's rudeness with a buttonholing smile for Deborah, to match the accent which said that we upper middle-class English have got to stick together. 'Alec's a very lucky chap—though he probably doesn't know it.' He came very close to Deborah, and his cornflower-blue eyes crinkled down at her. 'How long are you staying?' he asked.

'Two weeks,' said Deborah, determined that her glance should not waver.

'Do you water-ski?' and when she shook her head: 'fine, then you must let me give you lessons. You'll take to it quite easily, you know. You've the . . . right physique. Reduced rates for friends of the family, to coin a phrase.'

Gloria was making small movements of irritation, then vented her feelings on the boy. 'Alec! Stop fiddling about with that ski!'

Alec took his small foot out of the ski. 'I can nearly go on one ski, Miss Tarrant,' he said.

'He can do no such thing!' snapped Gloria contemptuously. 'He wailed and made my life a misery till I let him try it with the two joined skis that the beginners use, and the first time he flopped, he cried like a baby!'

Alec's lower lip hung sulkily, and he walked away, thin shoulders hunched.

'That boy!' muttered Gloria. 'He doesn't know the difference between truth and lies. The stories he tells me—honestly! He used to take me in at first, and the wild goose chases he led me on, and all. Once he bandaged his leg right up to the hip and said he'd broken it.'

'Young Alec,' pronounced Danny, watching Deborah, 'young Alec is one of those who eschew the old tag about truth being stranger than fiction. He'll back his foetid imagination against his slender experience of life any day.'

Deborah smiled in grudging rapport. 'I've learned *that* already!' she said.

They caught the chocolate-coloured, ramshackle bus at the end of the dusty road that led from the beach. Deborah had changed into a crisp linen dress which already seemed to be wilting like a scrap of old blotting paper in the baking heat of the Mediterranean afternoon. Alec raced down the aisle to a seat at the rear end of the bus and piped for her to hurry and join him, bouncing with excitement. The British tourists stared fixedly ahead and willed it not to be happening, but the Maltese craned their necks to smile at the boy, and then nodded companionably at Deborah; with an unexpected thrill of pleasure, she realised that they took her for Alec's mother.

A whistling boy conductor in a battered peaked cap and a see-through string shirt clanged a bell, and they set off up a winding, narrow road, through a barren landscape of grey rock and sand-dusted scrub; with gears grinding out every turn, and the spray of artificial roses nodding under the porcelain statuette of Our Lady which stood in a small niche over the driver's window with a pink lamp of adoration winking.

The road came out from between dry stone walls on to a plateau set with whirring steel windmills—and then all Malta was laid out before them: hill succeeding hill, in the heat haze, to an horizon of blinding blueness speckled with the white sails of distant yachts: and the compact shapes of towns stood like pieces of cut-out scenery in a child's toy theatre, crowned with proud basilicas.

Alec dug her in the ribs; with a shock she saw that his face was the colour of rotten fat.

'I feel a bit sick,' he whispered.

Oh my God, thought Deborah. She saw the English couple in the seat in front of them: red necks and freshly laundered linen—all unaware of their peril.

'Hang your head out of the window,' she said, wondering at her calmness in coping with such an alarming situation. Alec obeyed, and she clung on to his belt for safety.

He was still hanging there—tousled and happy—when they came to the outskirts of Valletta; and stopped to take on a pale young priest in a soutane, who gravely declined to take the seat which was humbly proffered to him by an old woman in black. And soon they were skirting the maze of harbours, and mounting the broad road into the ancient city of the Knights.

The walls of the side-street café were lined with bubbling, illuminated fish tanks, and Deborah had jibbed at going in because small fish alarmed her with their hostile watchfulness and their quickness, but Alec had squealed with delight and dragged at her hand.

Now they sat at a corner table, and he was slurping his way down a second, monstrous concoction of coloured water and bobbing ice cream. She smoked a cigarette, an untasted cup of tea at her elbow—and tried not to look at the myriads of unwinking, tiny eyes that regarded her from the green-shaded murk all round.

The café was air-conditioned against the cloying heat of the city streets, and the sudden coolness made her shiver in her damp dress. She saw that her fingers were trembling, and this brought her a new awareness of her vulnerability.

Had the awfulness of Diana's death left her in a state of nervous unbalance? Or was it simply that her basic temperament and lack of experience made it impossible for her to cope with the emotional gymnastics of a difficult six-year-old boy? Yes, that was it. The whole thing had been a ghastly mistake, and she never should have proposed the excursion. She'd only done it out of compassion for his waif-like appeal and his loneliness. Beware of pity, she told herself.

She looked at her watch: three-thirty, and the bus went at four. Roll on four o'clock.

It had begun so promisingly . . .

She directed back her consciousness, tentatively (the way a cat approaches a strange bowl of food: making small rushes, but baulking at contact). And then it all swam back in hard focus: the long, straight shopping street called Kingsway; one side in shade, and the other in broiling sunlight; white-uniformed American sailors, slouching and camera-hung; pink British and readily smiling Maltese. A party of whistling workmen with knotted handkerchiefs for headgear were putting up—or taking down, perhaps—street decorations for some religious festival or other: archways of painted flowers, tawdry-gay in the pitiless light.

Which way to the Knights' armour? A tall, white-habited friar stooped to hear her question, till she could see the frosting of sweat on his tonsured scalp. Straight on past St John's co-cathedral, turn right, and you will see the archway into the palace yard.

'Soon be there, Alec. Are you getting excited?' But Alec was making sucking noises with his mouth, and scanning the shops on the opposite side of the street. Then he jerked her hand.

'Miss Tarrant . . . there's a toy shop! Can we go across and have a look?'

'But, I thought you wanted to see the Knights' armour so badly.'

'I've got one-and-eightpence . . . and I want to buy a gun.'

Bemused, she let him be the leader. He nearly had them both under the high-stepping hooves of a pair of black horses drawing a carriage-load of grinning sailors, who whistled after Deborah.

She died a thousand small deaths of embarrassment in the toy shop, conscious of the anxious, hovering assistant as they both watched Alec's hands moving clumsily along the stacked shelves in a tactile exploration of miniature cars, airplanes, string puppets, mechanical grabs, military dolls for dressing, bijou playing pianos, plastic packets of beads, and Meccano sets—all indiscriminately.

'I thought you wanted a gun,' she said presently.

He stood jingling coins in his pocket, and pouting down at his sandals.

'It doesn't matter,' he whispered. 'I haven't got enough money to buy what I *really* want.'

'What *do* you really want, then?' she said, determined to keep the thing at a placatory level.

He shook his head, and his eyes were full of tears. 'It doesn't matter,' he choked.

'Alec . . . *please*!' she pleaded.

It seemed that he had noticed a display of underwater swimming equipment—big-eyed masks with snorkels, black rubber flippers, and deadly looking harpoon guns—and now he must have a pair of flippers so that he could swim faster than Danny. Deborah had a clear impression that the idea had just come to him quite out of the blue. They found a pair to fit him, and he stood like a delighted, small frog while she paid for them.

'Now for the armour,' she said.

But the way to the palace was a via dolorosa. He saw another toy shop where they had flippers which were more like the ones he wanted. Cakes on display in a window reminded him that he was hungry, and when would they be having tea? She had to wait for him outside a street urinal—anxiously, because he was a long time, and it seemed to her that she must have missed him—while men shuffled out past her, buttoning themselves: one said that he needed her, leering close, so that she could smell the tobacco and garlic on his breath. She was trembling when Alec came out and said he would like an iced lolly. He was still sucking it ("It's best to lick the part that melts down the stick, or you lose most of it") when he trailed slowly after her, up the baroque splendour of the marble staircase, under the stem eyes of the Grand Masters of the Order of St John in the paintings all round, to the vast hall, where the walls were hung with great cartwheels of uncountable weapons.

They walked among the glass cases with the suits of silent, empty armour. 'You were so right to want to come here, Alec,' she said, but he was probing the paper bag and peering in at his flippers. When they flopped on to the stone floor, she picked them up irritably and tucked them under her arm.

'I thought you wanted to come here more than anything!' she blazed.

'I'm hungry,' he whined. 'Is it soon tea time?'

Tea was another disaster. They went to a restaurant in Kingsway that smelt of freshly baked eclairs, and looked like a setting for a *thé dansant* from an illustrated magazine of the 'twenties. Alec would have this, and this, and this. It was all jolly scrumptious, he told her. But he soon pushed the plate away to play with his flippers again. No one had taught him to lay his knife and fork neatly side by side.

Afterwards, time-killing inconsequentially through the maze of backstreets, he stopped complaining about feeling tired to ask her if they could go to Gozo tomorrow.

'No!' grated Deborah savagely. 'I don't suppose there are any toy shops on a small island like Gozo, and they probably don't sell iced lollies either. So what would be the use of taking you?'

Soon after that, they found the café, blessedly near the bus station, with the walls lined with fish tanks.

She felt better now. Going over the thing in her mind had made it seem less frightful—amusing, even. Thank God she hadn't lost her sense of humour. But one thing emerged: she was not—emphatically not—temperamentally suited to the agony of traipsing a small boy around a strange city on a tropical afternoon.

She relaxed and drank her tea. The bus would be leaving soon. Her thoughts drifted pleasurably to her quiet, single-bedded room overlooking the bland, blue bay; a warm bath, followed by a lie down with a book before she dressed for dinner. Should she wear the blue silk Paisley, or the gold? . . .

Deborah came out of her reverie. The boy had finished his ice cream soda and was trying to fasten the too-large strap of a watch around his skinny wrist. It was a woman's watch; she caught the glint of diamonds on the miniature case.

'Alec, what are you doing with that?'

He thrust his lower lip out, sulkily. 'It's mine,' he said.

'Give it to me!' She took it from him. It was quite an expensive watch; the diamonds seemed real, and the case could only have been platinum. Turning it over, she saw the engraved name: *JENNIFER KEARLEY.*

'Alec, where did you get this? Did you pick it up somewhere in the streets today?'

'No. It's mine.' Sullenly. 'It belongs to me.'

Gone, the veneer of relaxation she had managed to lay over her tired nerve ends. Deborah had a vision of being taken to an alien police station with a wailing, small culprit. She had an impulse to slap him.

'Don't lie to me, Alec. Where did you find it?'

He hunched his shoulders and trailed a grubby finger down the frosted side of his empty glass. 'It's all part of my secret,' he mumbled.

'Secret?'

'It belongs to my dead body,' he said. 'I found it near my dead lady . . . it must have fallen off when she dropped down and died. Let me have it, please, Miss Tarrant.'

'You appalling little!' . . . she beat aside his questing fingers . . . 'How *can* you tell such barefaced lies?' Now she saw it all very clearly. 'If you didn't pick it up this afternoon, you must have found it lying around somewhere in the hotel. Unless . . .'

'I didn't steal it!'

His face was sick-white now, the way it had been on the bus, and his dark eyes were agonised beyond tears—they stared across at her like the eyes of a whipped martyr.

'Alec . . . I didn't mean that . . .' in a wave of remorse. But he was on his feet, and backing away from her.

'You were going to say I stole it!' He evaded her hands when she tried to touch his shoulders, mouthing the words in an outraged, shrill treble, so that the other people in the café, and the man behind the counter, turned to regard them with blank-faced awe.

'Alec . . .'

'You hate me, don't you? Like the others . . . like my daddy!'

'Alec . . . no!'

'My daddy never wanted a little boy . . . he wishes I was dead . . . and so do I!'

Then he was out of the door, squirming between an English couple who entered; leaving them staring up the narrow side-street at his small figure dodging between the slowly moving lines of traffic, so that Deborah had to push past them.

'Please . . . let me get after him!'

Across the wide road, plastered with glistening black rubber by the scudding cars, Deborah saw a curved sweep of stone balustrade; above that there was only blue sky and the white towers of distant churches.

She ran across the road, the way he must have gone. Somewhere, an army truck swerved on its screaming tyres, and a man shouted.

She leaned against the warm stonework, hand pressed against her heaving ribs, eyes closed. And when she opened them, she was looking down the dried earth of a public garden that sloped to the edge of an abyss. Below all that was a great void: the rock-walled canyon of Valletta's Grand Harbour, with its floor of shifting turquoise and emerald, and the white decks of anchored ships.

No one in the garden but the scarecrow figure of an old man stooping to pick up pieces of paper and fruit skins from amongst the wizened bushes. She shielded her eyes against the white glare, and panned the line of the wall that overhung the harbour.

'Alec!'

He was standing there, on the wall, looking down into the water far below him: a small brown skeleton of a statue to all the desolation and wretchedness of childhood.

She lost a shoe somewhere on the steps down to the garden; ran, stumbling, over the cracked earth, and the old gardener paused in his work to stare at her. When she came near, she kicked off the other shoe, moving slowly and quietly. Alec's back was turned to her, and he hadn't moved.

(Oh, God . . . don't let it happen . . . not *again*!)

Then the wall, chipped by wars and bleached white. Above her, the thin shafts of his legs, so close that she could see the delicate down on them.

She reached up with both her hands, praying for strength . . .

'Wheee! Look, Miss Tarrant . . . it's an American cruiser, and they're going to fasten the anchor chain to that huge buoy-thing. Look! Look! See the sailors in the little boat . . . two of them's jumped up on to the buoy-thing, and they're pulling the chain down on a piece of rope . . .

'Look at those big guns, Miss Tarrant. Look at them. Wheeee!'

Up from the abyss came the strident whine of electric generators, and a homely Texan voice blaring over a loudspeaker for libertymen to lay aft. Through her tears, she saw the white figures scurrying like lice in the floating city of dull, grey steel.

'Oh, isn't it *supersonic*, Miss Tarrant!'

Deborah wound her arms round the dancing, thin legs, and laid her cheek against the downy skin—so suddenly precious and beloved.

In the jouncing bus, the lumpy Maltese mum in the seat across the aisle had given Alec a pomegranate; she nodded and smiled as he chawed into it, munching the liquified flesh so that it poured from the corner of his mouth, and blowing out the pips with high disregard for Deborah's linen skirt.

'Is it nice?' asked Deborah, her arm round his shoulders. 'I remember my mother once bought me one from a fruit stall on market day, but I never found a way inside to the tasty bits. So like a honeycomb.'

'Smashing. It's smashing.'

'Alec. About the wristwatch: I promise I won't interfere, but *you* must promise to give it to Gloria when you get back to the hotel, so she can hand it in at the reception desk.'

He licked a carmine-stained tongue round his smeared mouth.

'All right,' he said. 'If you say so, of course I will. And you're going to take me to Gozo tomorrow, aren't you?'

She smiled down at the top of his raven-dark head. 'It's a date,' she said. 'Straight after breakfast.'

By the time the hotel came in sight, the humid heat had increased, and the South wind that blew from the open furnace door of Africa was massing slabs of black clouds over the islands.

CHAPTER 3

'Rain? You're not tellin' me you get rain at this time o' the year. Not in the blue old Med. now.' Thin and tall as a crane, grey hair slicked back in two wings over his ears, clipped moustache, white dinner jacket, red-black carnation, double-garage-suburban accent; a cad if Deborah ever saw one.

'Oh yes, sir.' The barman flashed gold teeth. 'I promise you we sometimes have much, much rain in September when the sirocco is blowing. It does not last long. A few moments' deluge. Whoosh. It is over.'

'Well, I'm not disposed to argue with you, old feller. Didn't put in any o' my wartime service with the Eighth Army wallahs, y'know. Never in the Med. area. Sent when ordered. Norway. Lofoten. Normandy to the Rhine, all that kind o' thing. But never in the Med. . . .' His rheumy, pale eyes connected with Deborah as she approached the bar, and explored the blue paisley dress . . . 'Evening, ma'am.'

Deborah assembled a withdrawing smile, and ordered a gin and tonic.

'Aaah, the little lady will have this with me, Frank.' And he affected not to notice Deborah's murmur of protest. 'Marker's the name, ma'am. Major Jack Marker. Very agreeable to have a spot o' glamour in the place on a dead night like this.'

Save for them, the bar was empty—as the dining room had nearly been. Wearied by her afternoon in Valletta, Deborah had fallen asleep after her bath, and it was past ten-thirty.

'Everyone has gone to St Julian's Bay for the feast day firework display,' supplied the barman. 'Three coach loads.' He went out through a door at the back of the bar, carrying an empty ice bucket.

Major Marker took her arm, squeezing the fleshy part above the elbow till Deborah's skin crawled.

'Saw you down on the old beach this mornin,' he breathed, in an odour of denture solution. This was obviously meaningful, and he regarded her quizzically. Without replying, Deborah raised her hand to her hair, and the movement of her arm disengaged his fingers. Wearily, it came to her that Major Marker reminded her of some of her mother's coffee-friends' husbands—the obliging ones who had been so useful with the lawn and the light fittings. At least her experience of men extended to being able to cope with the Major Markers of this world; there had been an "Uncle" Timothy, whose hand had sometimes insinuated itself round her waist with more than avuncular intent . . .

'Cheers, then,' said Marker, raising his whiskey glass to his cheekbone, and peeping coyly through it at her with one grotesquely-magnified, lubricious eye. 'Likewise chin-chin and tally-ho!'

'Your very good health,' she murmured.

Major Marker dabbed his moustache with a black silk handkerchief. 'Without wishing to bandy ladies' names around the mess, and all that,' he said, 'I observed one little filly who will have to look to her laurels now that you've arrived on the scene. I refer, of course, to la belle Gloria.'

'Gloria?' Deborah stared at him uncomprehendingly.

The major smoothed a wing of his hair with a little finger, and rolled his eyes. 'Who's lately been the monopoly of our friend Danny,' he said. 'But I observed Danny regarding you with a more than appreciative eye . . . and la belle Gloria with less than girlie-girlie chumminess. I think you may have trouble there, m'dear. *Latet angius in herba* . . . I don't need to translate, of course.'

Deborah nearly laughed aloud at the man's absurd impudence, but settled for raising a chilly eyebrow—and was completely misunderstood.

'But of course not. Of course not!' he said hastily. 'My most abject apologies, m'dear. The feller's not a gentleman. Jumped-up grammar school type. The ruination of the old country. No more than a hireling boatman, actually. Gel like you would naturally gravitate to chaps of her own style . . .' He moved nearer to Deborah, and his elbow slipped as it slid along the bar, and she realised that the gallant major was drunker than she'd thought . . . 'Chaps with the background . . . breeding . . . substance. Dare I say *maturity*?'

Deborah escaped behind her glass, so that his face swam through the clear liquid. She was saved by the return of the barman—and the arrival of a large woman with iron-grey hair, at the sight of whom Major Marker turned his back on Deborah and picked up a full glass from the bar counter.

'I've written four postcards.' The woman's voice boomed through the empty recesses of the room. 'Now I shall have my drink, and go to bed.'

'I have it for you here, m'dear,' said the major, and he sat with her, still with his back to Deborah.

The barman flashed Deborah a bullion-laden grin, and winked.

'I shall take a sleeping capsule tonight,' announced the woman. 'To facilitate sleep,' she added.

'I think it's a very good idea, m'dear.'

'You'll not be long?'

'Er . . . no, m'dear.'

'Good. I don't wish you to be long.'

Silence.

Deborah drained her drink, and picked up her handbag. On the way out, she passed close by the couple, and—with a wayward impulse of mischief: 'Good night, Major. I'll remember your warning . . . about the snake in the grass.'

Major Marker dropped his eyes, and his muttered reply was lost in the act of dabbing his moustache with the black handkerchief. His wife stared at Deborah in slack-mouthed affront.

Out on the terrace, the wind had dropped, and there was no sound but the beat of shingle on the shore line; the cicadas were still. The night sky was overcast, and Deborah felt her skin prickle with the clammy heat. The act of movement cooled her arms and shoulders, so she decided to go for a short walk.

An army camp of stone, flat-roofed barrack huts skirted the road that circled the bay. Apparently deserted, yet not quite deserted; she could hear the clatter of booted feet on asphalt; a couple of soldiers crossing a parade ground somewhere out there in the gloom. Then there came a laugh, a door slammed, and she was alone again in the night-stillness.

On the other side, the beach was hidden by a line of rhododendron bushes; up ahead, the seaward edge of a dark escarpment was broken by the stone watchtower on the headland. She decided to walk as far as the tower, perhaps half a mile.

She walked steadily, just fast enough to feel the air moving across her damp skin. Halfway round the bay, she turned to look back at the towering hotel, with the feast of lights at its base, and most of the bedroom windows darkened. Somewhere behind one of those windows, little Alec Rattigan lay asleep. She hadn't seen either the boy or Gloria at dinner, but he obviously ate quite early. What time are six-year-old boys put to bed nowadays? Did the nursemaid stay with him till he was asleep? Alec had told her they shared a room; she hoped Gloria didn't go out and leave him alone at night without making some arrangement with the floor maid to look in on him.

Deborah's heartbeats increased with sudden anger. What sort of father (she supposed there wasn't a mother—dead? divorced?) would send his child on an extended holiday abroad with such an obvious good-time girl as Gloria?

(Look, Mr Rattigan. I've grown terribly fond of Alec, and I can tell you that that boy shows every classical sign of lack of affection. He responds to kindness by being wayward and perverse; testing all the time to see if the love will dry up because of his naughtiness. A child without love, Mr Rattigan. Turning inwards upon himself. Building a fantasy life that can only be hinted at to adults with half-digested fragments of horror he's spelled out for himself from the newspapers . . .)

Deborah told herself that she was learning fast about small boys, and that tomorrow's excursion would be quite different from today's. Now she understood the wayward naughtiness, she could combat it with understanding and affection. Yes—affection—for since that scaring moment of relief at the wall above the Grand Harbour, she knew that there was a very special bond that joined her to the lonely, appealing little boy who had walked into her life only that morning.

The road took a final, flourishing curve at the end of the bay, and the watchtower was no more than fifty yards away, set back from the road on the first slope of the escarpment: square-cut and flat-topped, with a solitary, eyeless window in the soaring façade, and a flight of stone steps leading up to a deeply recessed doorway.

Deborah was abreast of the tower, was actually turning on her heel to retrace her steps back to the hotel when—it happened.

Starting from the zenith, the whole of the air and the landscape was burnt white; white from the jet-black shadows of a solarised photographic print; every pebble on the beach below, each wavelet to the horizon, the shrubs on distant hills, the hotel; all recorded so clearly in every detail that it seemed that she must be able to reach out and touch the texture of the whole world.

The light flickered and faded—then intensified blindingly, so that she covered her eyes and screamed.

The immediate thunderclap crashed out directly overhead, drowning her scream, and the rain followed: suddenly, and in drenching torrents, splattering muddy sand knee-high on the road, roaring in cascades from the stone gutterings at each corner of the watchtower roof high above her.

Instantly soaked to the skin, and buffeted by the weight of water, Deborah ran blindly—hands extended—towards the steps of the tower. Four steps up on hands and knees, and her fingers were scrabbling at the streaming woodwork, till they found a rust-roughened latch which clacked when she bore down on it.

The door swung open, and the second lightning bolt showed her an empty, high-ceilinged chamber—and then quenched it in blackness.

Nothing, now, but blackness. That, and the great roaring overhead, and a steady drip-drip on the stone floor.

(Calm. Keep calm. No need to panic. All you have to do is wait for the storm to blow over; the man said they never last for long. But it's so eerie in here. A light would help . . .)

Her handbag was a sodden lump, and she knew her lighter would never work. Then she remembered the window, and groped her way along the wall till her hand rounded a crumbling edge. When the lightning played again, she was looking out through the iron-barred window, across the bay.

The rain was still teeming down, but she was safe from its violence . . .

Another lightning flash. And this time something happened outside. Surely there had been a *movement* at the edge of her vision: something on the road, below the steps? She strained her eyes against the blackness, and waited while the thunder crashed out again.

Flash . . .

And, in the flash, she saw it . . .

A tall figure silhouetted in the road: the figure of a man, standing with legs splayed, tall and thin as a crane. He seemed to be staring up at her, and as she watched in sick horror, the bird-like arms flapped grotesquely.

Darkness again . . .

(Get out of this place. You're trapped. Trapped in here, with only one door, and a barred window too high from the ground.)

She edged back to the door. Her only escape. Leap down the steps, and run out into the night and the rain.

She waited, gathering the shreds of her courage, closing her eyes against the next flash—fearful that she would find the bird-creature already with her in the high-ceilinged chamber, with the door closed behind him, shutting them in together.

She touched the edge of the door. It was just ajar; she felt the rain beat on the back of her hand.

Now . . .

Out through the door, pulling it to behind her, with the rain like a whiplash against her face. Slipping on the steps.

Falling on her hands and knees to the bottom, and picking herself up.

The lights of the hotel were her guide. She raced towards them, past the dark curve of the rhododendron plantation; and the way back was a lung-bursting nightmare, with every step haunted by the terror of a thin hand that might close upon her shoulder . . .

She reached the hotel terrace, and leaned against a pillar, choking with relief and exhaustion.

No one saw her go in. Passing the window of the bar, she saw the barman with the gold teeth polishing glasses; there was no one else in there. The man behind the reception desk was reading a paperback; he never looked up as she tiptoed across the foyer on her bare feet, and ran up the stairs.

CHAPTER 4

The full-throated, woman's scream chilled the breakfast hubbub to shocked silence, and half a hundred faces turned on the instant. Deborah felt a spasm of physical terror, and knocked over a glass.

The stout woman was sitting alone at a table across the gangway from her: lobster-red face and shoulders above the pouter pigeon bodice of a bile green sun suit; hennaed hair and rimless glasses; a trail of liquid bacon fat trickled from slack, vermillion-smeared lips to the knobbly rope of beads at her jowelled neck.

'Eeeeeh! Take it away. Make the horrible thing go away!' she screeched, pointing.

Deborah dared herself to look, and smiled at what she saw. It was a minute, green lizard stuck to the tiled wall against the window a few feet from the woman. A band of sunlight brought out the delicate pattern of its smooth skin. Agate-eyed, it could have been a piece of cunningly fashioned costume jewellery; the rapid ripple of breathing was its only movement.

'Take it away. Somebody please take it away!'

Two waiters came running: laughing, joshing boys. They made great play of hunting the little reptile, flicking at it with the ends of their napkins, and exchanging quips in the harsh, glottal Maltese. And when the lizard had skittered out of the French window, they bowed like knights errant to the stout woman, and there was only concern and kindness in their guileless faces.

Deborah smiled as she dabbed away the puddle of spilled orange juice from her table top. The brief, absurd excitement had been cathartic, washing away the last detritus of the previous night's horror. She had—surprisingly—slept well, and awakened with a sense of excitement at the sunny, new day. Today she was taking Alec to the island of Gozo, and hysterical imaginings in the rain-drenched night were very far away. Yes, and the bird-creature image had been all her imagination, too, she had decided . . .

A man's voice from the next table: 'I'd hate to think how she'd have reacted if it had been a snake. It could very easily have been. I saw one in the hills yesterday afternoon.' Deborah had already registered him—disinterestedly—when she had scanned the restaurant for Alec and Gloria. He was mid-twenties, boyish-faced, with his hair stylishly *en brosse*. In spite of his pleasant voice, he was ever so slightly ingratiating, she decided.

'I thought there were no snakes on Malta,' she said. 'Didn't Saint Paul perform a miracle and get rid of them?'

'Legend says he got rid of the poisonous ones, or made them harmless,' he said. 'But even that falls short of the truth of the matter. There is still a mildly venomous variety on the islands.'

'You simply can't believe anything nowadays,' said Deborah.

He brought his coffee over and sat opposite her. They introduced, and he was Richard Needham—a schoolmaster. It turned out that he knew Southwold quite well, in fact his aunt owned a weekend cottage over the Blythe, at Walberswick. East Suffolk was lovely, and wasn't it a small world?

Deborah let him carry the limping burden of the conversation, looking round every time the frosted glass doors of the restaurant swung open. It was past nine o'clock, and still Alec and Gloria hadn't shown. Casting her mind back to the previous morning, it had been quite early—eight-fifteenish—when they'd come down in the lift together. Funny. Alec had seemed so eager about today's trip. Perhaps he'd forgotten about the whole thing, or didn't care all that much after all. She felt suddenly quenched.

Needham was waiting for a comment from her . . .

'I'm sorry,' she said, bemused.

'I was talking about holidaying with one's family,' he said. 'And how this is the first time I've ever come alone. Are you one of many, too?'

'No. I'm an only child.'

He grinned admiringly. Lucky you, he implied; but his looks spoke differently, and the account of the four sisters and three brothers who blighted his existence was told more in pride than ruefulness. 'I feel a bit like Prometheus unbound,' he said, 'not to be lumbered with those awful Needhams for once. Would you like some more coffee?'

She shook her head. 'No thanks.' And by way of encouragement, but with more than half of her mind on Alec: 'I can't begin to imagine how wonderful it must be to be part of a large family.'

'You have to fight to stay a person,' he said. 'Luckily, I was a middle child, the second oldest son. But poor old Jamie—Jamie's the youngest—he's mothered and smothered by his sisters, and slapped down at every turn by us lads. That boy's got a problem, by jove he has . . .'

She slid a glance at her watch, and let his monologue seep through her consciousness half-regarded. He was talking about himself now. There was something about a promotion: he'd just been promoted head of a department in a new school.

She summoned up a congratulatory smile; but he was self-deprecating in that caricature of Englishness favoured by his age and class: 'Bit of nepotism, really. My old man's a friend of a big-shot on the local Education Committee.' They both laughed.

It occurred to her, then, that Alec might already have had breakfast, and was waiting for her out on the terrace. She imagined him waking with the dawn, eager to be up and doing, the way children are on Christmas morning. She thought of Gloria, heavy-eyed with sleep and snappy with it, being nagged out of bed by her tyrannical small charge.

Her companion was asking her something . . .

'Mmmm?'

'What I meant was,' he said, 'I'm hiring one of Danny's dinghies this morning. And I was wondering if—well—you'd like to come along. I'm hoping to get as far as Comino.'

Her fingers tensed convulsively, driving the nails hard against her palms. Impossible to begin to explain to a complete stranger, over the ruin of a breakfast table, with a waiter loading a tray with dirty dishes at her elbow. She fought to find an all-embracing phrase that would hint at a general dislike of boats and water.

And then—*she saw the shadow of the bird-creature*!

The image of the thing was back-projected on to the frosted glass of the double doors by the sunlight streaming into the foyer beyond. The gaunt, elongated form of her waking nightmare. Looming monstrously larger as it drew nearer, with a curious, bobbing walk. Again she saw the bird-like, flapping arms, and—as the small head turned momentarily to profile—the nose was hooked like a falcon's beak . . .

Deborah was on her feet, dragging the edge of the table-cloth in her frantic haste, so that a plate fell and was smashed to fragments on the tiles—when Major Marker loped into the room, followed by his forbidding wife.

He cocked his head sharply to the crash of the broken plate, and his watery blue gaze fled away in embarrassment to meet Deborah's stare. The pair passed close by her, the wife moving like a full-rigged ship-of-the-line, her eyes glinting a broadside at the girl.

'Are you all right, Miss Tarrant?' said Needham, solicitously. 'You look as if you've seen a ghost, you really do!'

Deborah nodded dumbly, and then managed to say: 'I'm quite all right, thanks. Do you mind? I really must go now . . . I have to look for a friend.'

The manager was playing a game of patience with a pile of invoices; he looked up, and shed some of his world-weariness to see Deborah.

'Good morning, Miss Tarrant. Mail? Yes, there is some mail for you.' He took two envelopes from pigeon hole sixteen, and slid them across the counter with the tip of a fourth finger that had been grown sabre-long like a mandarin's.

Deborah had not been expecting any mail; she had not given her holiday address to anyone but the daily woman who "did" the house in Southwold. To her surprise, the uppermost envelope was clearly franked: Bradford—and was addressed in the spiky, Victorian hand which could only have been her grandmother's.

The manager was in no hurry to get back to his invoices. 'Are you having a nice time, then, Miss Tarrant?'

She remembered her errand, and cut short the chain of association conjured up by the envelope. 'Thank you. Yes. Have you seen little Alec Rattigan this morning—or his nanny?'

No, he hadn't seen either of them. He glanced back to the pigeon holes. They were Room thirty-seven, and the key hadn't been handed in, so they must still be around the hotel—probably up in their room. Here comes Maria the housekeeper, and she might know.

Maria had just come down the stairs with an armful of linen. She was robustly middle-aged and swarthy as a gipsy. Gold coins swung from her ears, and she flashed a white-toothed, volatile smile when the manager indicated Deborah, and launched into rapid Maltese. The smile vanished when she grasped the import of his question. She snapped a reply, pointing back up the stairs.

'Is anything the matter?' faltered Deborah, but they ignored her. They were both shouting now. Maria had dropped her burden and was facing him with hands on her well-corseted hips. Harsh baritone fought to rise above sonorous contralto, and he thumped the desk with the palms of his hands at every phrase. Suddenly he dried up, hunching his shoulders in submission. Maria had no mercy. She drove home her point with another complete verse, and then picked up her bundle. She rolled her eyes to Deborah, and her earrings danced. And then she was gone.

'What was *that* all about?' asked Deborah.

He avoided her glance; became interested in aligning two ballpoint pens side by side on the desk top.

'It appears the boy and his nursemaid have gone out,' he said.

'Out?'

'Out for the day,' he said. 'They must have taken the key. It often happens. People forget to hand them in, you see.'

She stood alone on the edge of the terrace, in the sun, and the cacophony of voices rose in a continuous, jangling sound from the crowded beach below. Out in the blue haze, a grey-hulled warship was nosing its way southwards, towards Africa. Suddenly she felt alone and agonisingly bereft—and this was ridiculous, because he was only a little boy she'd met on the beach, and what was she to him?

She pulled a deckchair into the shade of the terrace awning, and sat down, fingering the envelopes on her lap, and staring across the bay to the watchtower. That was something else, another cause for unease: she knew for certain, now, that it was Major Marker who had followed her last night; had slipped out after his wife had gone to bed, and trailed her to the watchtower, soft-footed, dodging between the rhododendrons perhaps . . .

She shuddered at the disquieting image.

The bright, brave hopes of her holiday in the sun were becoming overlaid with this unease: the spectre of a revolting, middle-aged predator—and now Alec's unaccountable rejection of her.

'Nothing,' she told herself aloud, nothing's gone right with me since Diana died . . .'

Absently, she thumbed open the top envelope; blinked wayward tears from her eyes, so that the words swam into clear view:

Dear Deborah,

I telephoned, and your woman told me you have gone to Malta, which we think is a sensible idea in the circumstances. It can't be very pleasant for you in that house alone, with the constant reminders of your mother and her tragic end . . . (The empty bed in the hotel room when I first came here—oh, Grandmama, there's no escape from the reminders!)

. . . we both hope you will come and stay with us for a protracted period when you return from your holiday. Cummings can come down and bring you here by road. Yes, this would be the most convenient way to arrange it.

Have you given any thought to disposing of the Southwold

> house? Your grandfather says that property in East Anglia is very buoyant at the moment (whatever that means) and it will fetch a good price. You won't wish to be burdened with financial matters whilst on holiday, but grandfather wants me to assure you that he will continue the allowance he formerly made to your mother. Or perhaps you have some notion of going into business. A boutique would be very suitable. Grandfather would be very willing to set you up . . .

Then the act of turning over the page revealed the corner of the second envelope. Deborah saw the name of the hotel printed there, and her grandmother's letter fell, unregarded, from her fingers.

The envelope was not addressed; just her name, written in careful, childish capitals.

'Alec!'

One sheet of hotel writing paper . . .

> Dere Miss Deborah Tarrant
> it was fish and chips for diner which was smashing and i dident see you ther. wasent it nice today at valeta and i hop it will be nice tomorrow i will be wating for you to go to gozo at eighto clock in the morening.
>
> yours truely
> Alec Hugo Rattigan esq

It was now nine-thirty . . .

Late-risers were still straggling down on to the beach with their sun-tan lotions and their copies of today's London papers flown in overnight. Joey in his baseball cap was doing his best to find a place for them all. He paused in the act of driving the shaft of a beach umbrella into the soft sand, and smiled shyly across at Deborah.

She called to him: 'Have you seen Alec?'

He shook his head.

A group of grave-eyed children were gathered round Danny and his two assistants, who were working on the outboard engine of a speedboat. The big man's hands were blackened to the wrist, and there was a smear of oil across his bronzed pectorals. His cornflower-blue gaze met Deborah's sandalled feet, and swam up the length of her sun dress.

''Morning,' he grinned, and went back to his work. The two Maltese boys nudged each other, eyeing Deborah, and started to wrestle, like young puppies.

'Cut it out, you two,' grated Danny. 'Let's get this bloddy engine off and switch it for the spare.'

'Have Gloria and Alec been down this morning?' asked Deborah.

Danny gave three turns to a butterfly-headed nut before he looked up again. 'No,' he said casually. 'At least, I haven't seen them. Should I have?' And then he seemed to register her expression. 'Is anything the matter?'

'I'm rather worried,' she said. 'Alec was to have met me after breakfast, and he's nowhere to be found. I thought you might . . . I mean . . .'

One of the Maltese boys sniggered. Danny shrugged his big shoulders and picked up a screwdriver. 'I'm not their keeper,' he said flatly. 'But there was some talk yesterday . . . Gloria said something about going to Gozo. I expect they'll have caught the ferry.'

'But Alec was to have gone with me!'

'Well, I know nothing about *that*.'

'You've no idea where they could be?'

'Not unless they've gone to Gozo, like I said.' He crouched, and clasped the massive bulk of the engine to his chest. 'All right, you two layabouts. Tear yourself away from the bird-watching and give me a hand with this thing. Mind your backs, everybody!'

Deborah watched the three of them manhandle the engine through the ring of onlookers towards a stone-built boathouse at the back of the beach.

'Mees Tarrant!' Running, hare feet in the sand behind her. It was the boy Joey. 'I hear what you are saying to Danny . . .'

'Yes?'

The effort of speaking to her gave him the most exquisite embarrassment; his smooth chest heaved breathlessly; the dark, pansy-soft eyes fluttered away from hers. 'I am thinking they cannot have gone to Gozo,' he whispered.

'Why?'

He swallowed hard. 'I came to work late thees morning . . . on the bus that goes to the ferry. There were four people from the hotel waiting at the bus stop . . . and Alec and Gloria were not weeth them, Mees Tarrant!'

The whine of a vacuum cleaner filled the third floor corridor, and the door of Room 37 was open. Through the inner door, a contralto voice was delivering a stream of angry invective in rapid Maltese. Three steps through the tiled lobby, past the bathroom, and Deborah saw the housekeeper Maria standing with a hand on hip, stabbing a finger at a weeping girl in a white nylon overall who was pulling back the sheets from one of the single beds. Maria's eyes flared in surprise to see Deborah, and then she smiled—but only with her lips.

'Were you looking for something, madame?' The gold coins at her ears danced as her head snapped round towards the quietly sobbing girl. 'Stop that noise, will you!'

Deborah felt at a loss before this formidable woman, and the uneasy premises forming in her mind were about to be revealed as hysterical imaginings—she sensed that.

'This *is* the little boy's room . . . and the nursemaid's?' she faltered.

Maria rolled her eyes and sighed. 'Yes, madame.'

'Well. I can't understand where they can be. It's . . . suddenly become a mystery. And I'm rather worried.'

Maria muttered something in Maltese, which drew a choked retort from the girl, who stood watching them. The older woman silenced her with a single, glottal word—and the girl broke into sobs again.

'All this talk of mysteries,' boomed the housekeeper. 'This one started it . . .' pointing to the girl . . . 'I say to you, madame, where are the mysteries? It's clear to me what happened. They get up early and go out for the day. What's the mystery in that? You can show me a mystery in that, madame?'

'I . . . I suppose not,' said Deborah.

Maria smiled approval, and her eyes softened. She took Deborah gently by the elbow, and they turned to leave the room together.

Deborah's foot sent something skidding across the lobby floor. Stooping, she picked up one of Alec's flippers—the flippers she had bought him in Valletta. Their touch brought her a sudden, ineffable sense of deprivation. She sensed that Maria was watching her as she hung the rubber flipper on a clothes peg by the door, beside a small grey macintosh.

They parted in the passage, and Maria's eyes crinkled good-humouredly. 'Your little friend will be back tonight. You'll see, madame. Don't worry.' She patted Deborah's arm. 'Have a nice day.' Then she disappeared into a room a few doors further along the passage.

When Deborah turned back to Room 37, the girl in the white nylon overall was standing in the doorway, the tears still wet on her cheeks.

'Maria is wrong,' she said brokenly. 'She won't believe me. But I know my own work.'

Deborah's heart quickened its beat 'What do you mean?'

'The beds. That girl . . .' she pulled her lips down in a moue of contempt . . . 'that Gloria. Is she the sort who would make her own bed and the little boy's?' She pointed inside the room. 'When I come to do the room, I find the beds made, and tell Maria about this. Maria say: "Lazy little slut, because guests make some kind of mess making their own beds does this mean you can pretend your job has been done, eh? Strip those beds and do them again!" . . .

'I refuse, and there is a big row. It . . . it has been like this all morning . . .' and she started to cry again.

Deborah noticed—without any surprise—that her hand trembled as she laid it comfortingly on the girl's shoulder.

'Please . . . what are you trying to tell me?'

The girl said: 'The beds were as I made them yesterday, don't you see, madame? I know my own way of making a bed. There was no need to do them again.'

So that was it.

'*Neither of the beds was slept in last night*,' breathed Deborah.

CHAPTER 5

Just after eleven-thirty, a call came through from Maria's Bar in Strait Street, to say that they were having trouble with a drunken sailor from one of the Yank cruisers, who swore that his wallet had been pinched, and would they please for God's sake send someone round in a hurry?

The whole business took Joe Borg, the duty inspector, two hours to straighten out, and he stayed at Maria's for a cheese roll, a hard-boiled egg and a bottle of Coke. He drove back to Cospicua through the lunch hour traffic and parked outside police headquarters in a spot of shade that should have lasted till he went off duty at six—always supposing he wasn't called out again.

He went in through the cool archway—slender and well-knit in his tan lightweight suit—and nodded to the two constables on duty. At the far end of the echoing, stone-flagged corridor, were the doors of the chapel with DOMINE DIREGE NOS sand-blasted on the plate glass. There was a dark-haired girl—English—talking to one of the clerks outside the C.I.D. office. Borg gave her a second glance and docketed her as twenty-five, attractive, Protestant, and probably lost her travellers' cheques.

The clack-wait-clack of Detective Constable Mike Agius's

one-finger typing came out of the open door of the duty officers' room to greet him. Agius's big, water-poloplaying back was hunched over the machine and his ankles and feet were twisted tortuously round the leg of the chair, to provide a purchase, in case the thing counterattacked perhaps.

Borg glanced over the curve of one massive shoulder. Agius had typed the heading in capitals, and was halfway down the page that was splattered with droplets of his own sweat.

REPORT TO DEPUTY POLICE COMMISSIONER ON PROBABLE MAFIA ACTIVITY IN MALTESE ISLANDS

Borg sighed. 'Man, you're obsessed with the damned Mafia,' he said. 'I shouldn't wonder if you don't look under the bed in case there's a Mafiosa lying in wait for you to go to sleep.'

Agius's young, bland, tanned, bovine face came up sullenly.

'Oh, you're back, Inspector,' he said. 'What happened?'

Borg peeled off his jacket and laid it across the back of his chair; sat down and picked up the daily report.

'No crime,' he said. 'The sailor was pretty far gone. Man, the hooch those fellows can get through in a hot morning. He'd been sick all over the place. Maria and that son of hers were shouting their heads off. He's a bad lot, by the way, that Amato.'

'I know him well, Amato,' said Agius. 'We were altar boys together at Lija. He used to steal our tomatoes.'

'Maybe, but he didn't steal the wallet for all that. The sailor had a couple of pals with him. They were telling him all the time that he'd left the wallet back aboard the ship, and only brought a few notes ashore in a paper clip. I helped persuade him that this was so, and we all ended up friends. The sailors sang God Save the Queen, and asked my name and address, so they could send me a card at Christmas. Anything happen while I've been out?'

Agius said no, and went back to typing his report, which was entirely unofficial, and based on the most sketchy conclusions, as Borg well knew from conversation with the earnest young detective. Borg bore the hesitant clatter for a few minutes, and was about to tell Agius to do the confounded thing—if he felt he must—in his own, and not the department's time, when the clerk came in.

'Young lady to see you, Inspector Borg. A Miss Tarrant.'

Borg recalled the girl he'd noticed on the way in.

'What does she want?'

The clerk looked embarrassed, and closed the door behind him. He rolled his eyes, showing the whites.

'Missing persons,' he said. 'She's reporting a boy and his nursemaid who've gone missing. But she could be another nutter.'

'Missing—from where?' asked Borg.

'From the Sunshine Hotel.'

'Bring her in,' said Borg. 'And give that typing a rest, Mike.'

He could be anything from thirty to forty, she thought. His hair was deep chestnut and sleeked back in wings over his ears, his face heavily tanned and scored with deep furrows down each lean cheek. The eyes were hazel and flecked with pinpoints of a darker tone—and they held her watchfully.

'Well then, Miss Tarrant. Supposing you tell me all about it?' In a well-modulated baritone, without a trace of accent.

She began—hesitantly—watching him for signs of reaction and getting nothing, conscious of how ridiculous it must sound to him.

She explained about her date with Alec, about his note, the mystery of the beds that had not been slept in, and all the time the flecked eyes never left her; he sat with lean, bare forearms folded against the whiteness of his shirt.

She wavered to a halt, feeling that there was more she should have said; something more conclusive, more tangible. He seemed to think so too.

'It really amounts to this then,' he said. 'According to the chambermaid—but not the housekeeper—the boy and his nursemaid didn't sleep in their beds last night.'

'The girl was quite definite,' said Deborah desperately. 'The housekeeper was determined that the chambermaid was trying to get out of remaking the beds, and she shut her mind to any other possibility.'

He inclined his head and sketched a gesture of doubtful acquiescence. 'Mmm, well, that's a point. But it's pretty much all you have to go on. If the chambermaid was mistaken, what we have is simply a case of a little boy who changed his mind and went out for the day with his nanny after all.'

'But he wouldn't do that!' said Deborah. 'Not after writing that note. He was dying for me to take him to Gozo.'

'The nursemaid may have decided to take him to Gozo. He wouldn't have much choice if she laid down the law.'

'No!' cried Deborah vehemently, and when his eyes flared with sudden surprise: 'she wouldn't take him out. She never took him out. All she wanted to do was play on the beach and be admired. She . . . neglected him shamefully. He was . . . is . . . a very unhappy child.'

One of his eyelids flickered slightly. 'Have you known this little boy for long, Miss Tarrant?' he asked.

'No,' she murmured lamely. 'I only came to Malta the day before yesterday . . .' her breathing quickened . . . 'but, in a strange way, I've grown terribly close to him, and I believe I understand him . . .

'Inspector,' she pleaded. 'I may be making a fool of myself, but isn't it worth making some enquiries? Just . . . just in case.'

Borg considered that for a few moments, then he got up, taking his jacket. 'I'll go back to the hotel with you,' he said. 'And we can probably clear up the whole tiling in half an hour. Do you have a car?'

'I came here by taxi.'

He opened the door for her, and when she went through, he grimaced to Agius. 'Ring through to the hotel if anything turns up,' he said. 'And don't waste all afternoon on that blessed report of yours. There's plenty of useful jobs you can be doing. Don't expect I shall be long. See you, Mike.'

'Don't forget you're supposed to be looking in at your aunt's place this evening,' said Agius.

Minutes later, Borg slotted his Triumph Herald into the stream of traffic that swooped down the curving road to Pieta and the north of the island, between the dusty tamarisk trees, with the sheer blue water of Marsamuxetto harbour below. Reaching up to adjust his rear-view mirror, he let it pan across his companion's face. She was nibbling the corner of her lower lip and her eyes were taut, staring ahead.

Definitely not a nutter, he thought. But there's *something* wrong there. Oversensitivity? Overimaginative?

He negotiated the tricky bottleneck at the roundabout, where the road leads off to Sliema and Ta'axbiex, and then he said: 'Don't worry about this business. I'm sure we're going to find a perfectly reasonable explanation for them not being around the hotel.'

'What worried me most,' she said, 'was this—sort of—conspiracy of silence.'

'How do you mean?'

'Well, both the housekeeper and the manager were unhelpful and evasive. And when I asked him to ring for a taxi to take me to the police station, he bacame almost unpleasant.'

Borg laughed. 'There's no great mystery about his motives for that,' he said. 'No hotelier likes to see policemen around the place, it makes the guests uneasy. As for the chap at your hotel—I know him well—Borg is a bundle of knotted nerve ends, the sort who grows ulcers about the Chinese situation.'

'Borg?' she said, surprised.

'No relative,' he said. 'Borg is the Maltese equivalent of Smith. If you called out "Borg" in Kingsway at a busy part of the day, you'd get a hundred replies. And quite a lot of them would be Joe Borgs, like me.'

That's better, he thought. She really is quite lovely when she smiles.

Then they were out of the towns that were strung like beads along the glistening black road—Msida, Birlarkara, Balzan—and into the countryside of pocket handkerchiefsized fields bounded each by the crumbling dry stone walls, where old women stooped with their hands in the rocky earth, and the steel windmills sang. Borg drove with a hand very near the horn; children, fowls and goats spilled with high disregard along the road edges and in amongst the squealing tyres. Horns shrilled at every corner, and once Borg had to back into the gateway of a field to allow a bus load of children to pass by: fluttering hands, and shrill laughter, and the tight smiles of nuns.

Deborah saw the horizon of the sea again, and the white bulk of the hotel above the beach.

'There's something else,' she said. 'Something I forgot to tell you. One of the beach boys saw the people from the hotel who were waiting to go to the Gozo ferry this morning, and Alec and the girl weren't with them. And they didn't order a taxi—I checked at the reception desk.'

'I don't think that's terribly significant,' said Borg presently.

'The hotel's fairly isolated, but they could have set off to walk and then begged a lift. Maybe even got hold of a passing taxi. No, I still think that the only real cause for concern is that their beds mayn't have been slept in.'

'The girl's quite adamant about that.'

'Well, we'll see,' he said. 'If she was mistaken, all your worry's been about nothing, hasn't it? The boy and his nursemaid will arrive back later today from Gozo, or Valletta, or wherever they've been.' He flashed her a grin that made his lined, brown face very boyish. 'And you'll have dragged me away from my siesta for nothing.'

She forced an answering smile.

'Not to worry,' he said. 'If we find them already arrived back, no one will be more pleased than Joe Borg!'

But they weren't back. Deborah knew that as soon as she saw the manager's face. He came out to meet them. The two men shook hands and began a rapid conversation in their own tongue. Deborah felt suddenly alienated from the calm, slow-speaking inspector. In Maltese he was someone else; shrill, volatile, unpredictable. And what were they talking about?

Borg broke off and motioned her to precede him through the door into the lobby.

'They're not back,' she said flatly.

'No,' he said. 'But he says that the chambermaid's changed her tune. We're going to see her now. Everything may be okay.'

The interview took place in the office behind the reception counter. Deborah sat by the window, and Borg perched on the corner of the manager's desk. There were children playing on the terrace outside: shrill cries, the thud of a ball, and the murmured chorus from the packed beach below.

The housekeeper came in, followed by the girl, who had been crying again. Maria preened herself at the sight of the inspector, making her earrings jingle. She pointedly ignored Deborah.

'All this fuss!' she shrilled. 'When will all the work be done today?'

The manager made a placatory gesture. 'It's all right, Maria. No harm's been done. We have to get this thing settled. If you'll just tell the inspector how Linda . . .'

'I'll have it from Linda herself!' said Borg brusquely. His voice softened, and he glanced encouragingly at the girl. 'Now then, Linda. This bedmaking. Was it yours, or someone else's?'

'Idle!' cried Maria. 'All this because she's idle. Idle and a liar!' And the girl burst into loud sobs, pressing her roughened hands to her face, so that the tears seeped between her fingers.

'Be quiet!' snapped Borg. He took a white handkerchief from his pocket, unfolded it, and gave it to the girl. 'Come on, Linda. Mop up, and tell me about it. Did someone else make those beds?'

'She knows that well enough!'

'Will you shut up!'

The girl wiped her cheeks, sobbing. And when she had her voice under control, she began: 'When I go to do thirty-seven this morning, I find the beds made, and start to strip them because today is Wednesday, and we change the sheets and pillowcases . . .'

Deborah felt a cold finger of shock trail its course from the base of her spine to her neck.

'Yes, go on,' murmured Borg, encouragingly.

Linda swallowed a sob. 'It's then I think that the beds were the way I make them, because there are little things I do, like tucking under the end of the sheet twice, over the pillows . . .'

'And you thought you recognised these small things in the way the beds had been made?'

Linda nodded vigorously, and blew her nose. 'Yes,' she said. 'But . . .'

'Go on,' said Borg.

The girl's eyes met Deborah's for a flickering instant, and then moved away. 'But . . . but I can't be sure, you see . . . by the time I think I have noticed these things, I have already disturbed the sheets, to begin changing them . . .'

'She's lying!'

Deborah was on her feet, cheeks burning, and all their shocked eyes were on her.

She faced the girl, shrill and accusing. 'I saw you in that room at about a quarter to ten this morning, and there was no *question* of changing the sheets. You told me . . . you were *sure* . . . that those two beds were just as you'd made them the day before, and you'd told the housekeeper that there was no need for you to do anything with them . . .' she turned to Borg . . . 'don't you *see*, Inspector? They've been getting at the girl!'

Borg's flecked eyes swivelled towards the manager, who sagged in his chair, mouth open, sweat running down the watershed of his brow.

'They're trying to hide something,' Deborah persisted. *'They know that room wasn't slept in last night, but they're trying to hide the fact!'*

At three o'clock, Borg phoned through to the C.I.D., and Agius answered.

'This is Borg. Anything happening?'

'Quiet as the grave. And you?'

'Man, I'm up to my ears in it.'

'The missing persons still missing then?'

'And how! Listen. Get on to Gozo and tell them to put all available men on to looking for them. Here are their descriptions—Alec Hugo Rattigan, English, aged six, height four-three, slim built, dark hair. Gloria Pritchard, English, early twenties, height five-six, good figure, attractive, red hair . . .'

'I like the sound of Miss Pritchard. She can come missing my way any time she likes.'

'Shut up, Mike! Listen. Gozo will be packed out with day trippers, and they could be on Ramla beach, or sightseeing in Victoria, or Mgarr, or God knows where. So it's a pretty hopeless prospect, but tell them to try. And, Mike . . .'

'Yes.'

'Tell them to put a man on the ferry point. And tell them to keep him there till the last boat leaves tonight. Got that?'

'What about you? Are you coming back here before you go off duty?'

A pause . . .

'I'm going to watch the arrivals of the Gozo ferries from this end. Well, hell, I'm off duty in a couple of hours or so . . . and I've sold Miss Tarrant the idea that it has to be Gozo or nothing, so I'm stuck with her. The poor girl's nearly out of her mind . . . did you say something?'

They sat amongst the sun-whitened rocks, on the slope above the road. Below them, the pier, where a cluster of dark-clad figures—Gozitans, homeward bound—waited for the next boat. What seemed like a stone's throw across the glassy blueness, the islet of Comino. In the distance, the stark cliffs of Gozo rising in their awful greyness from a drawn white line of breakers at their base; and the church-crowned hills rising above the hidden valleys beyond the cliffs. Above it all, illimitable blue sky.

Let him be over there, she thought. Somewhere on that island. Let me see him in the boat when it comes towards us. See him wave to me. If he's not there . . .

Borg flipped a stone down the slope and picked up another, tossing it in the palm of his hand.

'Another twenty minutes till the next boat,' he said.

'Mmm.'

He leaned back on one elbow, regarding her. 'There's really no good reason why those people back at the hotel should cover up, you know. Except that, if the two of them have gone missing, it would bring bad publicity to the hotel, and Borg wouldn't want to anticipate it by yelling from the rooftops that their beds haven't been slept in.'

'I suppose you're right,' she said.

He looked relieved. This was the way he wanted it, the way they all wanted it: that Alec and Gloria had to be in Gozo. She had half accepted the idea back there at the hotel. But the nagging doubts kept returning.

'I still can't see why Gloria should take him out today,' she said. 'Why should she, when she never has before?'

He hunched his shoulders and frowned. 'An impulse, perhaps. Pique. You took the boy out yesterday, and he came back babbling about the fun he'd had, and the fun he was going to have in Gozo with you today. Made her realise she'd been neglecting her duty. After all, he'll tell his father when he gets home, and she wouldn't want that . . .' he leaned back with a sigh of contentment, like a man who is conscious of having put a good argument . . . 'so she took him to Gozo, which was where he wanted to go.'

Deborah shielded her eyes and looked out to the far, grey walls of the island. 'And if they're not there . . . what then?' she said.

'Miss Tarrant, you mustn't . . .'

'No. Tell me.'

'We take steps,' he said. 'There's a routine procedure. I lay the facts before my chief, and he makes the decision. Once he's done that, the well-oiled machinery slips into motion. The person—or persons—become officially missing. All the island police alerted. Signals to all authorities in the Mediterranean area. Armed forces. Interpol. Commonwealth Office. New Scotland Yard. The lot. It's quite a schemozzle; like opening Pandora's box.'

She searched his eyes. 'And you don't feel like opening Pandora's box for nothing?' she said.

He shook his head slowly. 'Not on what we have so far.'

Numbly, her gaze returned to the beckoning cliffs. After a while, she murmured: 'He's a strange little boy. Though I feel drawn to him, I know so little about him. I wonder about the father; does he know quite how lonely Alec is, shut up in his childish world of fantasy? Do you remember the story of the children who kept lanterns under their cloaks at night; a warm light, private and alone, that only they knew about? Alec's like that, only the things he holds to himself, against the rest of the world, are complete fantasies. A body that belongs to him alone . . .'

'Come again,' said Borg.

'A body,' she said. 'A dead body.'

'Of a what . . . an animal of some sort?'

'No. A person. He has some fantasy about possessing a dead body of his own. He told me about it, as a secret, because he took a fancy to me and trusted me, I suppose.'

Borg smiled and shook his head. 'Kids!' he said.

Because it was connected, she had an impulse to tell Borg about the watch with the name engraved on the back—but decided not to. He was a policeman, however sympathetic. And Alec *might* have pilfered it.

The boat had come and gone again, and she had watched it creep away, across the glassy sea, trailing its fishbone wake.

She lay with her head resting on Borg's rolled-up jacket, her eyes closed, watching the blind discs of whiteness imprinted in her brain by the shut-out sun. The hard edge of despair was giving way to the new hope that he would be on the next boat. Nothing else mattered now.

Borg was talking. Reminiscing about his life as the seventh child of a family of twelve. Twelve small heads bowed in grace around a scrubbed table in a four-roomed house in a Valletta slum: huddling, barefoot and enraptured, on the front step, to see fireworks blossoming in the night over the high roofs: wax-candled feast days in the crowded basilicas, clutching at his father's hand when the sweating men swayed past with the great, painted statues haloed and crowned with gold. A young life compounded of desperate poverty and a limpid wonder at the beauty of familiar things. She decided that Borg must be, essentially, a very happy man.

He was unmarried, that much was plain. And he lived with his mother. Deborah assembled a Borg mother-figure in her imagination and she came out as one of the smiling, ageless, black-garbed women of Malta.

Mother . . .

The chain of association brought it all swinging back. She tried to fight it and—fighting—she was lost.

Diana was huddled in the bottom of the dinghy: a pretty little thing (strange how the phrase had persisted), grey haired, but still girlishly figured in her unspotted Lillywhites' sailing smock, new string gloves and shiny wellingtons. There was fear in the dolly-blue eyes.

'Deborah, I feel sick—and I want to go back!'

A descending slab of mist had blanked out the wavy line of coast from Southwold down to Dunwich. Spanked by the following wind, the quivering sails drove the small hull forward at an exhilarating pace. Deborah thrilled to see a limpet-crusted buoy flash past them, its chains creaking, and thought: damn her.

'You opted to come out with me!' she shouted, with the wind whipping her hair into her mouth, 'and now you're stuck with it!'

(And won't you make capital out of it at your interminable Saturday morning coffee parties with all your old biddies? How that graceless girl made you go out in her horrid little boat. You're hating this, my dear. It's the only element where you're no longer the mistress and I the slavey. Sick on, my dear!)

The older woman was crying now, and Deborah felt a surge of remorse. Away on the beam, through a hole punched in the mist, she saw a tall flagpost beckoning from the heights of Southwold—and she relented.

'All right. You win. Stand by to go about. Remember what I told you, and for heaven's sake don't lose your head and do anything silly.'

The frightened white face nodded obediently.

'Okay, then. Ready about—Lee-o!' and she gently eased the tiller to leeward. The sails flapped like a line of washing, and the small boat heeled in its turn. There was a scream from the huddled figure by the mast, and a string-gloved hand reached out wildly to grab for support.

'NO! Lie down flat—you'll have us over!'

Bet the onward thrust of fire beat was already scooping the grey water over fire side, and die thing was done and finished. There was no fear in Deborah's mind as the North Sea closed over her head. She registered is quite calmly—that the dinghy's buoyancy tanks would keep them afloat, and that they both were infated life-belts under their smocks.

Her head broke surface, and she whipped her hair from her eyes. The dinghy lay on its side with waves lapping ova its drewnod sails.

But no Diana.

She duck-dived, but it was impossible to sink far with the belt of air around her middle. There was nothing to see but dark green-greyness down there; when she raised her bead again, she was checking salt water from her lungs and screaming. And from somewhere away in fire were came death tell of a bell buoy.

It came to her then: Diana's nice new sailing smock had locked bulgy with tire belt inflated underneath; she hadn't noticed, it, and her mother would never have let on if she hadn't, blown un the belt before thay set off . . .

'Diana! Diana, where are you?'

Shocked awake, she sat up. The low-cast sunlight had darkened the sea, and fire cliffs of the far island were in deep shadow; against them she picked out a tiny speck of white.

Borg was staring at her in concern.

'You cried out, Miss Tarrant,' he said. 'You must have had a bad dream.'

She nodded.

'We'll get down to the pier,' he said. 'The boat's on its way here now.'

CHAPTER 6

He's not coming back . . . Alec's never coming back . . .

The singing tyres gave her the rhythm and tempo, and she made the words, staring blindly ahead into the sunset. They had not spoken since they left the pier. Borg's lean hand was just at the edge of her vision, capable, at the wheel.

Three more boats to come, yet, from Gozo—and an hour to kill till the next. Borg had said he must visit an aunt's house in Mosta (wherever that was). Something about a party. A party! She had stared at him uncomprehendingly, but the speckled eyes had softened reassuringly. She would enjoy it, he had told her. Just the thing she needed at a time like this, to take her mind off the worry of Alec. She'd said nothing—just got into the car. But now there was a whole world of distance between them.

The road was dipping, now, into the wide street of a town. People strolled the pavements in the coolness of the dying day: paterfamilias and their neat offspring; white-shirted loafers sitting round the open doors of the bars; children everywhere.

'Mosta,' said Borg. 'My mother's family all live here. Fine town and fine people. Many say they're the best of all the people in the islands. You'll see the dome of the church in a moment, and you're in for a surprise, I can tell you, Miss Tarrant.'

Ahead, a wide square. Johnnie's Bar. Working Man's Club—Liberty, Equality, Brotherhood. The Mosta Cycling Club. The Mosta Band Club. More men in their clean shirts and their neatly pressed trousers; shaved, pomaded and brilliantined for the long summer's evening of standing and regarding.

A bell tolled up on high, and she saw the towering dome rising straight from a circular base, flanked by two campinale, with a great Ionic façade and broad steps speckled with the dark figures of veil-headed women.

'There, now,' said Borg. Would you think to find the third largest unsupported dome in the world in a small town like Mosta?'

She knew he was watching her, gauging her mood, trying to re-establish the contact that had been lost between them, but she shrank away from it. The vast, manmade hill of honey-coloured stone slid past her vision, and she let it go, uncaring.

'Yes,' he said. 'Only Saint Peter's in Rome, and Saint Sophia in Istanbul have bigger domes than our church here in Mosta.' He spun the wheel, and they turned out of the square and down a narrow street between high-walled houses. 'Were nearly there . . . my aunt's place is quite near now.'

Another turn, and they were in a labyrinth of winding streets barely wide enough for the car to pass. Borg drove slowly. He flicked on his headlights, and the beam fingered the shadows, touching the bland faces of the people who sat on the steps at every dark, arched doorway. They moved through a jangle of beat music; in the dark cavern of nearly every house there was a bright television screen with the identical, flickering image of a youth with a guitar.

They crossed a minuscule piazza, watched over by a star-crowned madonna hung with bare electric light bulbs; then Borg brought the car gliding to a halt by a low wall overhung with prickly pear.

'Here we are,' he said. 'My aunt's house is just opposite.' He smiled at her in the gloom. 'Don't worry, Miss Tarrant I'll get you back to the ferry in time to meet the next boat.'

Light glistened through a glass-beaded curtain hung in the doorway, and her nostrils caught the scent of lavender polish and mimosa blossom as they stepped into a chequered-tiled hallway.

'Joe! Joe!'

They came clattering down a narrow marble staircase: two laughing girls in party dresses and high heels, dazzling with earrings and bright beads. They enveloped Borg, and he hugged their corseted waists.

'I've brought a friend,' he said. 'This is Miss Tarrant And these are my cousins Maria and Carmela.'

'Well, how nice of you to come. How nice, Miss Tarrant.' They squeezed her hands, and their dark eyes were full of sudden shy affection. 'We are very honoured to have you. This way, please.'

They led her up the stairs, and Borg followed. 'We can only stay for half an hour or so,' he said. 'Miss Tarrant has to go somewhere in half an hour.'

'Oh, Joe. Surely not!'

'Miss Tarrant, you mustn't go so soon!'

'But I must,' said Deborah. 'I have to . . . to meet someone from the Gozo ferry.'

They passed through an archway into a large, farmhouse-style kitchen, and a score of smiling faces turned to greet them.

'Joel Ah, Joel'

'And this is Miss Tarrant. She has to go soon.'

They closed in round her. It was hot in the room, and the men sweated cheerfully in shirtsleeves; the girls stayed cool in tight party dresses, and the women in corseted black.

'Oh, but you mustn't go soon.'

'You must have something to eat.'

'And a drink. What will you have, Miss Tarrant?'

'No. Come and see the baby first!'

'Baby?' Deborah glanced questioningly at Borg.

He hunched his shoulders and grinned. 'It's a baptism,' he said. 'A Christening Party. Didn't I tell you?' Then a giant of a man wrapped a black-pelted arm round his shoulders, and he flashed her a mock despairing glance as he was led away.

'Leave the men to their talk, Miss Tarrant, and come and see the baby.'

'This is our grandmother.' A tiny, bent old lady in black was arranging sweet biscuits on a plate. She cupped her hand to her ear and nodded up at Deborah with vigorous delight, breaking into a shrill spate of Maltese.

'Grandmother doesn't speak English. She says you are very welcome here, and that you are very pretty.'

One of the cousins took her hand. 'Come, please, Miss Tarrant. The baby is in here.'

In a small, silent room, a young woman was sitting on the crochetted counterpane of a bed, giving suck to an infant who lay cradled in her arms, cocooned in a white lace shawl. Three women in black stood as silent acolytes; and, from the bed head, a plaster madonna gazed down upon the delicate curve of the baby's cheek and the minute, perfect hand that plucked questingly at its mother's breast.

'This is Joe's friend Miss Tarrant. She's come to see the baby, but she can't stay long because she's got to meet someone from the Gozo ferry.'

It was a square-shaped flat roof surrounded by a railing, and they all sat around the edge, facing inwards. Overhead, a string of coloured lights, and beyond that the night and the stars. It was cooler outside, but some of the women fluttered fans.

Borg rose to greet her.

'Well, then. What do you think of the baby?'

'He's gorgeous,' she said. 'And fast asleep now.'

He took her arm. 'Come and meet everybody.'

There were more girl cousins, ranging from stout matrons to doe-eyed dollies; boy cousins with paunches and boy cousins in short trousers; Borg's eleven brothers and sisters; friends and neighbours.

'This is my Aunt Iris, whose house this is, and this is my mother.'

Two identical, smiling faces.

'My Joe must bring you to see me at my house some time, Miss Tarrant.' His mother was just as she had imagined her.

'That will be very nice, Mrs Borg.'

Later, Borg sat beside her, and the proud father of the baby—he was the big man who had buttonholed Borg when they arrived—pressed her to take a glass of sweet wine. Opposite them, a trio of the young girl cousins stole glances at her and whispered to each other breathlessly, smiling without guile when their eyes met hers.

'They're so pretty,' said Deborah. 'The three of them would make their fortunes as model girls in London.'

'Anna is a student nurse,' said Borg. 'Teresa is going to be a teacher, and Frances a mm. They'd be thrilled to bits if they heard what you had in mind for them.'

An old man came with a tray of dainty macaroons. He told Deborah to take two, winking and nodding encouragingly. He had the face of a Phoenician, leather brown and scored with a maze of wrinkles.

'I'm not really hungry,' she whispered to Borg.

'I know,' he said. 'You took them to please the old chap. I appreciate that. They're very simple, warmhearted people—and they like you very much.'

'I'm glad,' she said. 'I like them too. What a wonderful family you have. Your cousins took me into a bedroom where all the baby's presents are laid out I've never seen anything like it. Just like a film set. A satin counterpane, all hand embroidered. Crystal chandeliers. Everything gleaming and polished like a shrine; I felt that I ought to take my shoes off, and I'm quite sure I could never sleep in there for fear of disturbing its perfection.'

'No one ever sleeps there,' smiled Borg. 'It's the best bedroom. Only ever used for very special occasions, like this—or when one of the family dies and we all file in there to pay our respects.'

A glass fell and shattered on the tiled floor, suddenly silencing the chatter. There was a thin, high wail of anguish; and they all rose like wraiths and swarmed round a small figure that knelt beside the patch of wetness and broken shards of glass.

One of the women screamed; and the men's voices were hoarse with alarm and urgency.

'Oh, my God,' said Borg. 'He really has hurt himself.'

It was one of the ubiquitous small boy cousins. His mother clung to him, agonised, as the men swooped to pick him up. His shocked, white face was screwed in a simian mask of pain and terror. Deborah felt her stomach turn at the sight of the thick, arterial blood that spurted from his thin palm and splattered in heavy, dark streaks on the shiny tiles.

Borg thrust past her, dragging at his necktie, and shouting in Maltese. A moment of bewildered hesitation, and the men obeyed him, laying the screaming child on the floor again. Borg dropped to his knees and ripped the shirtsleeve, revealing the boy's thin arm, round which he hitched his tie, looping it and dragging it tight.

'Doctor Gauci!' rasped Borg over his shoulder, and one of the men ran out.

The flow of blood checked, and Borg gently prised open the boy's palm. The cut ran across the mound of the thumb in a single deep furrow.

Borg pressed the small head against his own chest, dragging the boy's horrified eyes away from the sight of his wound. 'It's all right, Manoel,' he murmured. 'Just take it easy, old fellow, and Doctor Gauci will be here in a minute, to make you as right as rain.' He looked up to Deborah, face strained. 'Can I borrow your handkerchief, please?'

She gave it to him, and he carefully tied it over the blood-smeared hand. Then he picked the boy up in his arms and carried him into the house, with the mother clattering beside him, and the others following, reacting the scene of the accident with gestures and loud, excited cries.

Later, in one of the bedrooms, Deborah and Borg stood together and watched a gentle-faced old man in pince-nez suturing the wound with a needlewoman's expertise. Young Manoel had recovered his spirits; seemed even proud of his exploit; he perkily responded to Doctor Gauci's joshing comments. And when the old man had finished, he gave the boy a sweet and tousled his hair.

Deborah met Borg's gaze and saw the relief there.

'We'd better get back to the ferry,' he said quietly. And she nodded.

When they got outside, he took her hand to cross the dark road; and when they reached the car, he did not release it at once, but stood there, silhouetted against the light from the curtained doorway of his aunt's house.

'Don't worry,' he said. 'Whatever happens . . . we'll find Alec. Please believe me.'

'Yes, I believe you.'

Two hours later, as they stood together on the empty pier, she had only his promise to cling to. Everything else was desolation: wavelets lapping forlornly against the piers; the damp night wind from Africa that brought no coolness to the skin; the unconsoling stars; the last ferryboat that had come and gone, and was now no more than a pinpoint of red light, bobbing over the dark sea towards the distant island.

Joe Borg delivered her back to the hotel and drove straight to headquarters. He paused at the C.I.D. office and looked down the dimly-lit passage to the chapel, where the red lamp of the tabernacle glowed thinly through the engraved glass doors.

He walked down the echoing corridor, and pushed open the door. Dipping his finger into the stoup, he crossed his brow with a droplet of the cool water; and sat down, burying his face, wearily, in his lean hands. Presently, he got up, genuflected, and left the chapel.

Detective Sergeant Nicholas Dimech and Detective Constable Carmel Bonnici were the night-duty officers, and they were playing two-handed whist with dummy partners. They looked up when he came in, surprise turning to amusement, and amusement to concern when they saw his gravity.

'Well, it's Joe! Can't you sleep, Joe?'

'What's up?'

'We've got trouble,' said Borg. 'And I think it may be serious. Will you put a call through to the chiefs home, please, Bonnici?'

Within the hour, Pandora's box was open, and the news was singing through the night.

CHAPTER 7

She was coming up; rising through layer after layer of the storm wrack, every layer getting lighter. And the bell buoy was sounding out above her head.

She gasped into consciousness. The pink telephone was jangling stridently on the bed shelf, and she reached out to take it, overturning the two-coloured sleeping capsules in their plastic tube.

'Miss Tarrant?' It was Joe Borg. 'It's just on nine-thirty. Are you all right?'

She brushed a strand of hair from her eyes, and found that her hand was trembling. 'I've just woken up,' she said. Everything was crystalising into shape, and with it came the crawling dread. A light breeze rippled the curtains, and she shivered. 'Is there any news?'

'No,' he said briskly. 'I've just checked with the hotel, and they haven't shown. But things are moving. Look, the boy's father's been contacted, and he's flying in on the lunchtime plane. Do you want to . . . I mean, would you come along with me to meet him at the airport?' There was a note of appeal in his voice.

'Yes, of course,' she whispered.

'Good, then. Go and get yourself some breakfast, and I'll pick you up about twelve. And, Miss Tarrant . . .'

'Yes?'

'Don't worry. It's going to be all right.'

She shrugged out of her damp nightdress and swayed blindly into the bathroom. The needle stabs of the cold shower shocked her drugged mind to a higher level of awareness, and she kept the water running till her skin ached. She met her own eyes in the mirror. They were dark-ringed and haunted, and her lips were slack with fear. But Borg had said it was going to be all right. She must hold on to that—so there was eye make-up, and bright lipstick to hide behind; the mockery of brightly printed holiday linen to mourn in. Oh, Alec . . . let it be all right with you!

There were piles of luggage in the hall outside the lift; a party of new arrivals from England, white-skinned, filed in from the sunlight and gathered round the reception desk, where Borg, the manager and two girl assistants were dealing with them. When the manager saw Deborah, he whispered something to one of the girls and rushed over to her, taking her elbow and walking with her to the door of the restaurant.

'Good morning, Miss Tarrant. I do hope you slept well. Oh, what a shocking business. The C.I.D. were on the telephone to me just now, and I had to regretfully tell them that the little boy and his nursemaid had still not come back here. They asked me to fix a room for the father, you know. He's arriving this morning.'

'Yes. I shall be there to meet him,' she said dully.

'Will you?' The news seemed to add to his unease. 'Why yes of course. You are very closely concerned.' They came to her table, and he pulled back the chair, snapping his fingers at the boy-waiter lolling by the serving hatch. 'Now, what would you like for breakfast, Miss Tarrant? The haddock is very nice. Fresh from Scotland. Or a little mixed grill would be very nice, perhaps. Sausages, bacon and all the trimmings.'

Her mind was screaming for him to go away and leave her. 'Just a cup of coffee,' she whispered.

Notepad in hand, the waiter stared uncomprehendingly at the manager.

'Coffee for Miss Tarrant,' shrilled Borg. He watched the waiter's retreating back, then flashed a glance round the room. It was nearly empty. Three tables away, Major Marker was eyeing them round the edge of his newspaper, while his wife ate with hers propped against the teapot before her.

The manager gave an embarrassed cough and said: 'I'm glad I was able to have a little word with you, Miss Tarrant—er—before the morning had progressed too far, as you might say. This business . . .' he sketched a gesture of despair . . . 'a thing like this could cause great unhappiness amongst the guests . . .'

Deborah drew a shuddering breath before she could trust herself to speak. 'If you're asking me to say nothing about what's happened,' she said, 'I can tell you it's quite unnecessary. I don't want to talk about it to anyone. *Anyone!*'

His dark face was washed with relief, and he made a little bobbing bow, backing away from her. 'Believe me, I'm so grateful, Miss Tarrant. Very considerate. I'll leave you now, to get on with your . . .'

She turned her head to the window to hide the sudden tears that pricked her eyes. The beach crawled with people, and a skier was cleaving a white wake behind a racing speedboat.

Oh, Alec . . .

'I have been following the Middle East situation with close attention the last few days . . .' came the booming voice of Mrs Marker . . . 'and I am of the opinion that a conflagration is imminent.'

'Yes, m'dear,' replied the major, one eye on Deborah.

* * *

She saw his grey Triumph Herald from the terrace, coming down the road that circled the bay, between the barrack huts and the rhododendrons. There was another man in the passenger seat. She rose to meet them.

'You know Detective Constable Agius,' said Borg, and the young policeman's eyes crinkled with pleasure. 'Well, if you're ready, we'll get off to the airport.'

Agius stayed behind. As Joe Borg spun the wheel and slammed into second gear he said: 'He's going to work on the manager now. By the time Mike's finished, we'll know the reason for all the shenanegans about the made or unmade beds.'

They came to Luqa airport. In the waiting hall, darkeyed children played tag around the seats, where their families sat in bovine patience with hand luggage and paper bags of food. Borg buttonholed a lovely, proud-walking Malta Airlines girl, who told him that the flight from London would be ten minutes late.

He took Deborah's arm. 'Time for a drink,' he said. I expect you could do with one.'

They sat in the bar on the upper floor, at a table near the balcony overlooking the apron. White-overalled mechanics were crawling over the wing of a two-engined aircraft with Arabic script strung out like butterflies along its fuselage. A fire wagon was parked near the road leading to the runway, and the man at the wheel was scanning the horizon to the north through a pair of binoculars.

She started as Borg touched her hand. 'Relax,' he said. 'Relax and drink up your drink. It's not time yet.'

The touch of the chilled lager on her tongue made her shudder.

'His full name's Mark Hugo Rattigan,' said Borg, avoiding

her glance. 'We understand he's a lecturer in Law at London University. Apparently he's a widower. That's about all we know.'

'Poor little boy . . . poor Alec,' murmured Deborah.

Borg stared down into his glass. 'Yes,' he said. 'That would explain a lot, wouldn't it? The things you were telling me—about his air of loneliness, his fantasy world and all that.'

'What about the girl,' she said presently. 'Aren't any of her people coming?'

Borg shook his head. 'An orphan,' he said. 'They managed to locate the convent home where she was brought up, and the Reverend Mother asked to be kept informed. But no—there won't be anyone coming to Malta on her account.'

An orphan. Deborah tried to assemble an image of Gloria in institutional dress; waif-like in a crocodile of pale children. But all that came out was the flame-haired Venus on water skis, laughing into the sun.

Borg hunched his shoulders, and drew vertical lines down the frosted side of his glass. 'I'm very glad you've come,' he said. 'It helps a lot, your knowing Alec. You'll know what to say to the father.'

(Shall I, though? Try it. Try a variant on the little speech you composed the other night . . . "Now see here, Mr Rattigan. You sent that child away, out of your sight, with a perfectly worthless creature, and he's been eating his heart out with loneliness and lack of affection. And now he's gone, Mr Rattigan, and it could be that you'll never see him again . . . never be able to reach out and take that warm little body in your arms . . .")

Then she was groping in her bag for her handkerchief, and Borg was trying to comfort her, speckled eyes clouded with compassion. People began to get up from the tables all round them, and a loud speaker crackled:

'Malta Airlines announce the arrival of B.E.A. Flight one-nine-six from London . . .'

'He's here,' said Borg. 'Chin up.' They joined the throng descending the stairs, past a framed painting of The Madonna of the Airways; to the sound of jet engines that rose to a screaming crescendo out on the apron, and then whimpered away to silence. Mark Hugo Rattigan had arrived. Chin up.

They stood together at the barrier screen separating the waiting hall from the customs area. Five minutes later, the first of the new arrivals rushed out: spry-eyed and hefting suitcases; calling to their friends and relatives. A young priest was engulfed by his mother; the father of a family was borne off by his laughing brood; a mini-skirted English dolly flew into the arms of a bronzed boy. The trickle became a steady flow—but not one of them could have been Mark Hugo Rattigan. Don't hurry yourself, Mark Hugo. It's only a little boy you've lost. Take your time.

And then she saw him . . .

His resemblance to Alec brought a sick lurch to her heart: Alec's shock of unruly black hair; the same spare frame, filled out to lean tallness; dark eyes staring.

Staring . . .

A Maltese porter was carrying his case, and guiding him by the elbow; but that hardly seemed necessary—Mark Rattigan managed very well with the aid of the white-painted stick that quested the edge of the screen door, the corner of the barrier and—briefly and gently—the toe of Joe Borg's shoe, when the detective, after a sharp glance at Deborah's shocked face, stepped forward and touched the blind man's sleeve.

'Mr Rattigan is it, sir? I'm Detective Inspector Borg, and the young lady with me here is Miss Deborah Tarrant, who's a friend of your son.'

His hand was cool and firm in hers. The eyes were unbelievably alive and perfect, though heavy with sleeplessness. There was a night's stubble around the strong mouth and jaw.

'How do you do, Miss Tarrant. It's very kind of you to meet me.' The eyes wavered towards Borg. 'There's no further news of Alec, is there, Inspector? You would have told me first thing.'

'No, sir. I'm afraid not.'

The loud speaker grated above their heads: '*Will Detective Inspector Borg of the Valletta C.I.D. please come to the telephone at the reception desk? Thank you.*' It was repeated in Maltese.

'That may be news,' said Borg. 'Wait for me here, please. I'll be right back.'

Then they were alone together, and her mind was fighting to readjust to the unexpected factor of his disability. She felt bereft; gauche. She looked at him. His knitted silk tie was slightly crooked, and he couldn't possibly know about it. She had an impulse to straighten it, but it seemed a futile gesture in the face of his air of utter relaxation—the calm strength of the blind.

'I've come as rather a surprise to you.' He was smiling.

'Yes,' she admitted.

'Alec didn't speak of me?' His deep voice carried an overtone of wryness, but it was soon gone. 'Of course not. He'd be much too concerned with the business of winning your hand. Did he ask you to marry him? He often does, particularly if the young lady's pretty. Are you pretty, Miss Tarrant? You sound as if you might be.'

'We got—we get on very well,' she said, disconcerted. 'He actually let me in on one of his dread secrets.'

'Oh, those dread secrets,' smiled Rattigan huskily. And he turned his face away from her.

He loves Alec, thought Deborah. He's dying inside . . .

Borg came back, elbowing his way through the crowd. Deborah searched his face for signs, but there was nothing but official blankness. He glanced at his wristwatch, and checked with the clock on the wall. 'Something rather urgent's come up,' he said, 'and I have to leave you. Will you both take a taxi to the hotel? and I'll be along later.'

'Is it . . . Alec?' faltered Deborah.

Borg shook his head.

Borg left his car at the end of the dirt track, and walked up the stone-strewn hill. A yellow lizard flickered away from under his feet and vanished amongst the grey scrub. The sun was high and scorching; he had taken off his coat, but carried it over his shoulder because it could often get quite chilly down at sea level, and the job might take all afternoon.

He crested the rise, and looked down on the sea, and the rock shelf below, where a couple of young boys were fishing with sea tackle. There was no sign of Mike Agius and the boat.

He slithered down to the shelf and stood at the top of the steep stairs cut into the living rock, with the deep blue water sluicing its bottom steps.

'You want to buy fish?' asked one of the boys, and when Borg shook his head: 'are you Sirens or Neptunes?'

Mike Agius played reserve for the Sirens water polo team. 'Neptunes,' said Borg gruffly. 'A boat's supposed to be meeting me here at the steps. Have you seen one around?'

'There were boats around this morning,' said the other boy. 'It was flat calm this morning, but look at it now.' He pointed down. The great saucer-like swells were smacking against the base of the cliff forty feet beneath them; wetting the rock wall, then retreating and baring its barnacle-plastered mystery below. 'You won't get many boats out in this.'

Then it came bobbing round the beak-like prow of the headland, and Borg saw Mike Agius waving to him from the bows.

The hunched figure at the tiller would be Charlie Cassar the postman, who ran tourists round the coast in his time off.

'The steps are slippery,' warned one of the boys.

He slithered halfway down; clutched at the smooth walls to right himself, and his involuntary shout of alarm echoed hollowly in the deep cleft. The boat came in sight below, rising and falling alarmingly on the swell. Mike Agius was scrabbling to pass a line through a rust-pitted iron ring. Borg did the rest of the steps on his backside; slithering over the green slime, and pitching head-first into the bottom of the boat with Agius's strong hand round his belt.

'Let's go, Charlie!' The engine roared, kicking them away, and the boys waved down at them from above.

Borg settled himself gingerly on the thwart behind Agius. The young constable was staring ahead, and there were lines of strain round his mouth. He isn't looking forward to this, thought Borg.

Charlie Cassar waved to him from the stem, nodding and grinning under his frayed-brimmed straw sombrero.

'Hello, Joe! I heard about your cousin's baby. Big boy, eh? What weight?'

'Nine pounds.'

'That's good. Takes after his father!'

They were heading southeast, a stone's throw from the unscaleable cliff that stretches almost the entire length of Malta's southern shore. Away on their right, Fifla islet: a broken tooth rising out of the blueness, target of a million shells from long-gone warships, and home of a unique species of lizard. Ahead, the crawling crests of the great swell that dashed itself to oblivion against the petrified sandstone bastion.

The boat was rolling heavily now, with bare inches of freeboard to spare. Agius crouched with a hand on each gunwale, shoulders bowed, a perceptible yellowness showing under the bronze of his thick neck. Borg decided to leave further questions till later.

They skirted close by another headland—perilously close, because the back-spray from the wall stung Borg's cheek, and he could see a shoal of small fish rising and falling against the rock—and came in sight of the cavernous mouth of the grotto in the centre of a shallow bay. This was their goal.

Charlie Cassar eased the engine and turned the boat towards the gaping archway; standing up in the stem with the tiller arm between his knees, simian face wrinkled as he peered ahead. 'Yes, I reckon we can just about get in,' he shouted.

'I'm on your side, Charlie,' grated Borg, taking a tighter grip on his thwart.

Closer, pitching heavily now, with the sea rolling underneath the boat. Closer, so that the clifftop overhung them, and they were nosing straight for the centre of the vast arch, with a big roller under their keel, driving them on. Then the roller was spent and thwarted against the pillars of the arch, and what was left of it was just enough to carry them forward into the cathedral vault of the grotto, with Charlie Cassar's shout of triumph echoing all round them, and blueness everywhere.

Blue like the lapis lazuli of Our Lady's mantle, thought Borg. An iridescent, sight-shattering blueness beyond believing; from the dark hue at the tips of the stalactites high above them, to the deep luminosity of the great basin of water in which their boat rose and fell in the muffled ground swell; in the reflected diamonds of sunlight flickering on the walls about them. Nothing but blueness—and bass organ-pipe groan of the sea.

They peered over the side. Mirror-clear in the blue cave bottom, they could see each shifting grain of the sandy bed, and the translucent tips of the stalagmites. A shoal of fish appeared black, shielded from the light—and then they turned and flickered away, suddenly silvered.

'See anything down there?' said Borg.

'There it is!' croaked Agius, pointing.

There was a bundle of old rags lolling in the swell at the base of the cave wall. Countless small fish nosed against it. As the three men stared, it rolled over, and a slender human arm waved like a white snake.

'Get the boathook, Charlie,' said Borg.

They brought her out, and Gloria's streaming, flamelike hair was violet-coloured in the blue light of the grotto: laid her in the bottom of the boat in the pathetic finery of the silky dance dress that was her shroud. Borg covered the head and shoulders with his jacket, to hide the purple skin that bulged above and below the cruelly knotted stocking round the throat—and everything else.

'Eyes are always the first to go,' muttered Charlie Cassar. 'The crabs soon go for the eyes, you see.'

CHAPTER 8

It was after four o'clock when a patrol car delivered the father and Deborah Tarrant to headquarters. Borg broke the news to them in the lounge adjoining the C.I.D. canteen, and was glad to leave them there together, having warned the canteen manager to keep everybody out. Mike Agius was just putting down the phone when he got back into the office.

'Nothing yet,' said the young constable. 'Every available patrol launch is out They're doing the south coast, starting from Marsaxlokk and on up to Comino. That was Fort Angelo—the minesweepers are just leaving Grand Harbour, and the Yank destroyer that came in this morning's due to follow them. The choppers from the carrier have been airborne since the word go, of course. Everyone's rallying round a treat.' Agius seemed to be enjoying it now, but Borg remembered the agonised retching when they'd pulled the girl's body into the boat. 'What do you think—do you think they'll find the boy?'

'You mean, do you think they'll find his body?' growled Borg.

'Well . . . yes, I suppose so.'

'Yes. I do.'

He sat at his desk and drew his lean hands across his face, wearily.

'What about the blind chap—the father,' said Agius. 'How's he taking it?'

'No way of telling,' said Borg. 'He's not the sort to show much, but that's not to say he isn't bleeding inside. He's upstairs now with Miss Tarrant. God, I'm glad that girl's around,' he added vehemently, 'it's a hell of a thing to be hanging over the head of a blind man!'

A lorry rumbled past outside, rattling the plastic slats of the Venetian blinds. Borg sighed and sat back.

'All right, Mike. Let's see what we've got so far. What about the couple who discovered the body in the first place?'

'They're outside in the waiting room,' said Agius, flipping open his notebook eagerly. 'I've got the basic facts here . . . David Richard Needham and Henrietta Milner; both in their early twenties; met at the hotel. They hired a sailboat from Danny's Ski School . . . and, by the way, I've got an angle on that chap Danny . . .'

'Save it . . . go on with the discovery of the body.'

Well. They left the beach about ten o'clock, with packed lunches from the hotel, with the intention of picnicking on Comino, but the wind was northwesterly, and Needham—who's not much of a sailing man—wasn't able to make much headway with his tacking in that direction, so he took the easy way out and made a long reach down the coast.'

'In the direction of the grotto.'

'Right. The Milner girl had heard about the grotto, and when she spotted it, she let out a squawk and asked Needham would he sail them in there. It was pretty calm this morning, of course, but Needham made a bit of a hash of getting in—biffed the bows against the side of the arch and scraped the paintwork. It was while they were panicking to get the sails down that the girl spotted the thing in the water . . . the body.'

'They went straight back?'

'If they'd had to sail, they'd still be coming. But they got a tow from a motor fishing boat. I was at the hotel when they arrived. The rest you know. Do you want to see them now?'

'Later. Tell me the rest . . . tell me how you got on with Borg.'

Agius smirked like the brightest schoolboy in the class. 'Man, I gave him a hell of a time,' he said. 'He was sweating badly when we arrived, so I waded straight into him—told him point-blank that the police believed he was hiding something. I went right through all the stuff about the beds again. He wanted to send for that tough egg Maria—to hide behind her skirts—but I wasn't having any. In the end, he crumpled and told me all. Well . . . he didn't spell it out in so many words, but I got the message.

With accuracy and detachment . . . scrupulously avoiding any pre-judgement,' said Borg wryly, quoting from the Police Training Manual. 'So—what was the message?'

Agius grinned coyly. 'The girl Linda was speaking the truth, all right,' he said. 'When she went into Room thirty-seven yesterday morning, she found the beds hadn't been slept in. And not for the first time, either—not as far as Gloria's was concerned, at least.'

'I get it,' said Borg. 'Who's the guy . . . Danny?'

Agius looked disappointed. 'Yes,' he said sulkily. 'The two of them have been carrying on ever since . . .' he checked with his notebook . . . 'ever since Gloria and the boy arrived two weeks ago, on the twenty-second of last month.'

Borg got up and walked over to the window, hands in pockets. A donkey barrow piled high with green melons was rattling down the cobbled street past the building, with an old man perched asleep, his head bowed over the animal's swaying rump. Borg supposed the donkey knew the way home. 'What do we know about Danny?' he said.

'Full name, Daniel Harcourt,' supplied Agius. 'British. Doesn't have residential status, or a work permit, but covers himself by skipping over to Sicily at the required intervals like a lot of them do. Rents the ski and boating concession from the syndicate who own the hotel.'

'Lives where?'

'Has a flat in St Paul's Bay. But—and this is why Borg and Maria became so sensitive when Miss Tarrant started probing—he also has the use of one of the staff bedrooms on the top floor of the hotel.'

'For entertaining his lady friends,' said Borg. 'Of whom Gloria Pritchard was the latest. And he squared Borg and Maria—which could get them both the sack from the hotel syndicate if it came out.'

Agius nodded.

'But what worried little Linda,' said Borg slowly, 'what worried little Linda, was the fact that the boy's bed hadn't been slept in either.'

'Right. What do we do . . . get Harcourt in?'

'No,' said Borg presently. 'I'll go and see him. After I've had a word with the couple who found the body.'

'I'll wheel them in now,' said Mike Agius, getting up.

He paused at the door, and his guileless, unformed face was working overtime on being shrewd. 'Man, I wouldn't be surprised if there wasn't a Mafia tie-up in this business,' he said.

'Tell me about it some time,' said Borg.

Waiting . . .

The human state, the seven ages of man—or woman: moist-palmed outside the headmistress's study the day you were sent out of the examination room for making a whispered reply to a neighbour's frantic query; staring through your tears at the television, with ears strained for a phone call from a boy who would never ring; sitting outside the coroner's court with the solicitor, the day they held the inquest on Diana . . .

There would be others: a specialist's waiting room, perhaps, while he pored clinically over the X-ray that would tell him all he needed to know; and there would be the last act of all—the long, slow wait for oblivion . . .

But now there was this. All life was going past in the street outside, in the sun. Everyone was so kind: Borg; the little man who looked after the canteen, who had brought them tea and biscuits; the two young policemen in the patrol car which had fetched them both here. Tonight, the life in the street would die down, and they would all go back to their homes to wait for another day just like this. But perhaps not Borg. No—she remembered his handclasp in the darkened street outside his cousin's house—he was *involved*.

She glanced covertly at Mark Rattigan. He was still sitting in the wicker armchair by the window, the shafts of sunlight through the Venetian blinds striping his impassive face. What was he thinking? Did he wish he were a whole man, with eyes to join in the massive search that was taking place for—she flinched at the image—what would almost certainly be the remains of his little boy, his only child?

'I've never seen him, you know,' he said suddenly, so that the unexpectedness of it made her heartbeat quicken. 'I was blind before he was born.'

She nodded, conscious of the absurd inadequacy, but unable to conjure up a word or phrase in reply.

'They sent for me in the night.' He seemed to be speaking to himself, thinking aloud, as if she were not there. 'I remember it was very cold. November. The hallway of the nursing home smelt of pine, and the matron was there to meet me. I caught the odour of her fear above the pine, and I knew something was badly wrong. She told me nothing then, and I didn't ask; just followed her down a long corridor to a small, hot room where a baby was screaming. The woman took my hand and guided it so that I touched something moist and warm; an assemblage of delicate flesh and tiny bones that could have been a small animal, newly killed and skinned, except that it moved . . . and it was a baby's shoulder and arm . . .'

She stared at him, not knowing what was coming, but dreading it.

'She told me he was premature, but quite perfect. She said it wouldn't be a good idea to pick him up. And all the time she was looking at me—the blind can always tell, you know—and trying to master her fear, but losing, so that in the end I had to ask her. And then she cried, and that was strange—don't you think?—because one would expect a woman who'd given her life to nursing would be made of tougher fabric than that . . .'

She was biting her knuckle now, not breathing, willing him to stop.

'His mother . . . my wife . . . was already dead when they'd sent for me.' He said it quite flatly, head bowed. 'And then the poor woman made this awful gaffe. Asked me if I wanted to see her for the last time, and that made her cry again.'

Someone came into the next room, the canteen, and he was whistling cheerfully. The sound stopped abruptly as if he'd been given a signal to be quiet. Deborah allowed herself to exhale, controlling it so that Rattigan should not hear. And long minutes passed in silence.

And then, briskly: 'They tell me we're very alike, Alec and me. Would you say that, Miss Tarrant?'

She swallowed hard. 'Yes . . . yes, I would.'

'Yes. That's what everyone's been saying in the last two

or three years,' he was speaking conversationally now, like someone passing round family photos. 'Till he was about three, he favoured my wife's side of the family. They're all dark, like me, but inclined to be shortish. I suppose, when he began to shoot up and outgrow his clothes, the presence of the Rattigan genes became more marked. Yes, that would account for it, don't you think?' And, without waiting for her to reply: 'do you know why I sent Alec to Malta for a holiday, Miss Tarrant?'

'No,' she whispered. His manner—which had become slightly hectoring—gave her a sudden unease.

'I'll tell you. It's really quite an absurd reason. Last year, and in previous years, we went on holiday together, to Bournemouth. It used to work out better than you'd expect, with a blind man and an active small boy. But Alec's grown up a lot, and last year he was bored with me, and I with him. So . . . I decided to pack him off with a nursemaid. But to where? And here's the absurdity. It was like picking a horse for the Derby by an association of ideas. One day, someone rattled a tin under my nose and said would I buy a flag for the St John's Ambulance Brigade? And that was a tip, you see, because the Maltese Cross is the symbol of the St John's . . .'

Shocked to compassion, she got to her feet. 'Mr Rattigan . . . please . . .'

'Can you think of anything more absurd, Miss Tarrant, than that a human being should have the tenacity to be born posthumously, battle through the million hazards of infancy and childhood, and then be killed on a sandstone outcrop in the middle of the Mediterranean because someone rattled a tin? . . .'

'No! Stop torturing yourself. It isn't your fault!'

She let some time go past, then laid a hand on his shoulder. Quietly, now, she said: 'It really isn't, you know.'

'Would it have happened if I'd been here?' Challengingly.

'You met Gloria Pritchard, and must have formed a pretty fair impression. Did she neglect the boy? She came from a highly regarded agency, recommended to me by the boy's regular nanny, who wasn't really up to making the trip with him. I didn't like her voice, but Alec seemed to take rather a shine to her. She was rather sweet to him, the only time I was around when they were together. I suppose she was keen to get the job.'

There was no point in concealing the truth. 'She was worthless,' said Deborah. 'I was quite willing to hate you for sending him away with her.'

'Oh, my God,' he said.

She looked down at him. Somehow, she thought, I should be able to reach out in the dark and touch this man, because we feel the same things; or is there a mutual repulsion between two people who know guilt and remorse?

Oh, Alec . . . oh, Diana . . .

Diana Tarrant's husband was killed in 1942, when she was six months pregnant, and Deborah's earliest recollection of her mother was of a pretty, helpless little thing whose dolly-blue eyes misted whenever people mentioned Daddy: who always had plenty of obliging big men on call when it came to such things as mending fuses or mowing the front lawn of the shabby little Georgian house with the bay windows looking out from South-wold's heights over the grey North Sea which was to destroy her.

Everyone thought Diana was wonderful. Didn't she bring up her fatherless little girl and keep the house going? Of course, it was generally known that Simon Tarrant hadn't left her well-provided for, for all that the Tarrants owned a chain of old-fashioned grocer's shops in the West Riding, and the grand-parents visited twice a year. Twice a year, their hearse-like Rolls was to be seen parked for the afternoon outside the run-down Georgian house, with a uniformed chauffeur asleep at the wheel. It was always assumed that they left a reluctant cheque behind when they departed, because the visits always coincided with the times when Diana settled some of her long-outstanding tradesmen's bills, and appeared at the Saturday morning coffee parties in a new get-up. Poor darling Diana, purred the Southwold matrons—serene in their own security—scrimping and scraping to keep up appearances, and having to beg her child's rights from those two grey-faced old fossils twice a year.

Deborah remembered her grandparents' visits: the dark, shapeless clothes and the alien-sounding north country accents; her mother shrill and nervous before they came. There was always a half-crown for Deborah, and then she was sent out to play in the garden, where she never strayed far from the long window into the drawing room, with a glimpse of the tall, gesticulating figure of grandfather, and Diana with her head bowed over a scrap of handkerchief on the sofa. It has seemed to her, then, that they were a pair of ogres, who came from a black never-never land in their funereal coach, to torment her mother.

The truth of it came to her much later—and it never came to the matrons of Southwold. On their son's death, the old Tarrants had settled fifteen hundred pounds a year on his widow and daughter: more than sufficient to maintain the pair of them in comfort—had it not been for the fact that Diana was hopeless with money. Not extravagant, nor a spendthrift; no secret drinking, or expensive boyfriends. Simply by carelessness and ineptitude, money dribbled away like sand through Diana Tarrant's well-kept fingers; and when it was gone she lived on credit. And by the time the old Tarrants' twice-annual visits came round, the credit was always wearing thin ("I'm sick with worry about money," was a phrase Deborah had been brought up with, and it always had the power to make her feel queasy), which was why she had to beg more from her in-laws—and she despising them as she did, because of their accents, and the fact that they were "only trades-people," whereas her own father had been ex-Indian Army.

Secure in her role of the brave little widow, Diana imposed on everyone—and particularly on Deborah. In her daughters case, this took the form of what Daddy would have or wouldn't have wished if he'd been alive . . .

In the matter of education, Daddy would have wished her to attend the snobbish little private school run by two faded spinsters, where Deborah learned the names of the books of the Bible by rote, and to say "thank you for having me"; where her natural talents were quietly allowed to atrophy like sprigs of fern between the pages of an old book. Deborah, who—as a child—had a lively head for figures, and a curiosity about the nature of things, left school at sixteen, apparently useless for anything but following in the wake of her mother. There was to be no "career" for Deborah—Diana made this quite plain.

Then there was the memory of the first and only boyfriend. She was seventeen at the time: tall and sturdy-limbed, with straight, mousy hair, and a determined chin that contradicted her gentle recessive personality; which reflected her father's family. His name was Evan, and they met on the beach. His skin was very white, and his shy gaze made her aware, for the first time, of her womanliness. Hugely daring, she had delivered the ultimatum to her mother, and Diana had been disarmingly co-operative, even insisiting on helping to buy the long dress for this—her first—dance. When Evan called for her, Diana wore a frilly hostess gown and poured sherry for the three of them. She waved them on their way—with a firm injunction that Evan must come in for a coffee when he brought Deborah home. She meant it, too, as Deborah well knew, and was waiting up for them. It had been a farewell coffee for Deborah and her Evan, as they sat and sipped miserably: she with her guilt, and he with his resentment at her flurried rejection of his tentative physical advances made on the way home to coffee and Diana. And when he'd gone it was a relief, because Daddy wouldn't have approved at all; not with a Cockney accent, a clip-on bow tie, and those *terrible* fingernails . . .

Daddy . . .

When Deborah was older, she tried to peel the mask from the ubiquitous Daddy, but there was only the photograph of the absurdly young man in naval officer's uniform in Diana's bedroom, and that was only like looking at herself in a mirror: the same bland eyes and deceptively determined chin. There was no other evidence unless you could count the thing hanging from the ceiling of the Imperial War Museum in Kennington. She had gone there in a taxi, on an impulse, when she and Diana were up in Town one day; left Diana under the hair drier and arranged to meet her for tea in Simpson's. The beery old attendant to whom she'd made known her requirements had led her into a vast hall and pointed to a mute, winged monster of painted-flaked aluminium suspended above them: in this—or something like it—her father was supposed to have plunged, a flaming torch, into the Mediterranean, while she was quickening in Diana's womb. But it didn't make any sense. Had Icarus cared, or not cared, about clip-on bow ties?

Her question unanswered, and having no defenses, Deborah resigned herself to being the gauche appendage of her pretty little mother whom almost everyone in Southwold admired. No life for her beyond the confines of the Georgian house, the genteel café in the high street, and occasional shopping trips to London; twin-sets, tweed skirts and a string of "good" pearls—and only the memory of a boy's white skin for make-believe when she kissed her pillow.

And so it might have stayed, but for the legacy . . .

Six months before, a remote Tarrant great-aunt—whom Deborah never met—died and left her two hundred and fifty pounds, a windfall which had coincided with an influx of demands from local traders. Diana was currently worried sick about money, and blithely assumed that the two hundred and fifty would fall into her delicate hands. But Deborah had other ideas.

Dolly-blue eyes brimming with tears of reproach, Diana had listened unbelievingly as her tall and suddenly alarming daughter informed her that she was to buy a dinghy and teach herself to sail—and, what was more, intended joining a sailing club to meet people. And she was only slightly mollified when Deborah proposed spending the remainder of the legacy on a fortnight's holiday for them both in Malta. This was also to be in the nature of a pilgrimage, explained Deborah, because Daddy had been killed fighting a convoy through to Malta in nineteen forty-two.

In the event, Diana Tarrant—like her husband—died at sea without ever setting eyes on St Paul's gentle islands.

When Borg came in, Deborah was standing by the window, and Mark Rattigan's eyes were closed as if in sleep. The blind man's head flickered round at the sound of the opening door.

'Any news, Inspector?'

He sounds calm enough, thank heaven, thought Borg. 'Nothing, sir,' he said. 'I'm on my way now to the hotel, but I just remembered something Miss Tarrant told me yesterday.' He looked questioningly at Deborah, indicating Rattigan. 'Perhaps she'd like to come down to my office . . .'

'It can be said in front of me, whatever it is,' said Mark

Rattigan evenly. 'Don't add to your labours by concerning yourself about my feelings.'

'Very well, sir.' The flecked eyes met Deborah's. 'It's the business of Alec's fantasy, the one about the dead body. Can you recall exactly what he told you, word for word?'

'I . . . I'll try,' she said. And she was back again on the beach, with the surf making islands of her feet, and Alec sitting hunched with his skinny arms circling his calves. 'He said he knew quite a lot about dead people because he had a dead body of his own, that he'd found. Yes—and no one else knew where it was.'

'Just that . . . no mention of whether it was male or female, this body?'

'No,' said Deborah slowly. 'I'm quite sure he referred to the body as "it"' . . . she gave a sharp intake of breath and stared at him in alarm . . .'you don't think, surely? . . .'

'Yesterday, it was a fantasy,' said Borg. 'Today—after what's happened—it could be something very different! Listen, now, Miss Tarrant. Think hard. Is there anything else even remotely connected with this supposed fantasy; anything he said, or did, that might give us some further indication?'

She nodded. 'Yes, there is . . . something.'

'Go on.'

'He had a watch with him, the afternoon we went to Valletta. A woman's watch. Gold, with a gold expanding band, and the surround of the face was set with diamonds. It looked rather expensive. There was a name engraved on the back. I asked Alec where he'd got it, thinking he'd probably found it on the beach perhaps. He got quite snappy; said it belonged to his dead body . . . *yes!* . . .' she saw Borg's mouth tighten . . . 'I remember now . . . he said it belonged to his dead *lady*! Only that bit slipped my mind till now. We had . . . a rather disturbing scene after that.'

'Do you remember the name on the back of the watch?'

'Yes. Jennifer Kearley.'

Borg wrote it down. 'Every little helps,' he said.

'I should have told you before,' she said.

'It didn't matter before. Probably doesn't signify anything now. But we'll look into it.'

He went over to the door. 'I'll give you a lift back to the hotel,' he said. 'Or would you rather stay here? If there's any news, it will come straight to the C.I.D. office.'

Deborah glanced at Mark Rattigan, and he nodded. 'We'll stay here,' she said. And then, as he opened the door: 'Inspector Borg, there's something else . . . something else Alec said to me on the beach that first morning. Rather macabre.'

'Yes?'

'He said it was wrong what they say in books—and that dead bodies don't smell at all.'

Borg nodded thoughtfully, and went out.

Borg went from the hotel to the beach, where half a dozen kippered forms were still trying to coax another layer of patina from the low-cast sun, and the beach boys were gathering up the chairs and furling the umbrellas. The ski boats were hauled up on the shingle, and the dinghies nodded at their buoys, sails flapping.

He stopped by the boathouse, and tried the door. It was locked.

Danny was down by the water's edge, bulky in the top half of a track suit. He turned with an expression of something very like fear to see the slight figure of the detective.

This was at half-past six. Deborah and Rattigan stayed at police headquarters till ten o'clock when—there still being no news—they took a taxi back to the hotel.

By that time, Daniel Harcourt had achieved the uneasy status of a man assisting the police in their enquiries—in the bland euphemism.

CHAPTER 9

It was still dark. Early morning delivery lorries ground their way up the hill into the city, and he saw the blinking lights of an airliner sweeping low to land beyond the heights of the Addolorata cemetery across the harbour. Borg took off his jacket, and walked slowly for coolness' sake; past the palm-fringed bulk of the Hotel Phoenicia and the silent fountain in the square; under the noses of the green bronze cannon outside the Auberge de Castille, and into the narrow canyon of St Paul's Street. Outside the covered market, they were working by harsh lamplight; unloading green melons, boxes of fish and the flame-heads of flowers.

He went into a café beyond the market; took his coffee and brandy to a table in the corner, away from the crowded counter; and slipped the duplicate sheets of typescript from the envelope he had brought with him. The top copy was now lying on his chief's desk, for him to read first thing . . .

INTERVIEW WITH DANIEL HARCOURT, CONDUCTED BY DET. INSP. J. BORG

Q. When was the last time you saw Gloria Pritchard?

A. On the beach. Yes, on the beach late that afternoon. I packed up about six. She was still there when I left.

Q. What did you do then?

A. I drove to St Paul's, changed, and had a few drinks at a bar, with a snack supper.

Q. Yes. And then?

A. (pause) All right. Yes. I came back to the hotel.

Q. What time would that be?

A. About ten-thirty.

Q. Dinner would have about finished in the hotel dining room by then. You didn't see Gloria and the boy around?

A. No. I wouldn't expect to see Alec. He'd be in bed. And Gloria had probably gone out, po thought. Or she was up in her room, washing her hair perhaps.

Q. I see. What did you do then?

A. I went up to my room—the room I have on the top floor. I had a few drinks, and lay reading a book till about twelve. Then I put out the light and went to sleep.

Q. I see. Just that. You stayed up in the room, drinking and reading a book. No one came in to see you, not Miss Pritchard or anyone else. You were on your own till morning. Have I got that right?

A. Yes, that's right. My reputation as a stallion's greatly exaggerated, Inspector. Sometimes I go to bed just to sleep.

Q. I'm sure you do. Now let's go over that again—you say you last saw the girl on the beach. You packed up the ski-school at six. Drove to St Paul's. Returned to the hotel at about ten-thirty and went straight up to your room. After a few drinks and a read, you went to sleep . . . what time did you say that would have been?

A. About twelve. Yes, that's how I spent the evening. If you'd like to have that typed out, I'll be glad to sign it and . . .

Q. All in good time, sir. Just a few more points. Do you know a girl named Barbara Farrugia?

A. I don't think so.

Q. You probably don't know her by name. She's a waitress at the hotel. Hasn't been there long. But maybe you've seen her around. She's about seventeen, medium build, glasses. Not a very pretty girl, perhaps you'd think.

A. Oh yes. So?

Q. I've a statement from her here. I'll read it to you, a part of it: "It was about a quarter to eleven, and I'd cleared my tables. I went up to the room I share with Ella Peregin and Sheila Micallef. On the way, I saw the little boy's nursemaid. She didn't see me. By the time I reached the top landing, she was going into Mr Harcourt's room." Now, that doesn't square with what you told me just now, does it, sir? What's the truth of it then?

A. (after a pause) All right, Inspector. She did come up to see me. But I didn't kill her.

Q. No one's said anything about that. So you admit that Gloria visited you at about a quarter to eleven, is that right? How long did she stay?

A. About half an hour. Perhaps a bit longer.

Q. What did you talk about—what did you do?

A. Do I have to go into that?

Q. No, it won't be necessary. But while she was with you, did she mention anything about a watch—a watch that Alec might have found lying around somewhere?

A. No. Nothing like that.

Q. Does the name Jennifer Kearley mean anything to you?

A. (without hesitation) No.

Q. About your boats, Mr Harcourt. The ski-boats first of all. Could anyone have started up one of those boats and driven it away that night without anyone hearing it in the hotel?

A. A ski-boat? Oh no. Those damned engines wake the dead. I'd have heard it myself, up in my room.

Q. What about the dinghies—there are three of them, aren't there? Where were they positioned that night?

A. They were drawn up on the beach. The weather forecast wasn't any too good, you see. And, of course, we had a thunderstorm.

Q. Were the sails on them?

A. Yes. They were furled—with the canvas covers on.

Q. Mr Harcourt—how long do you suppose it would take for a man to get the sail covers off, and drag a dinghy into the water and away all in the dark? Ten minutes—five?

A. No more than five, I shouldn't think. If the chap really knew what he was doing . . .

There was a lot more; the questioning had gone on for five hours. Borg read it through again, and drained his second cup. Not much to go on. After his first big lie, Danny had hardened his story and was sticking to it. Perhaps Sergeant Dimech could shake him; Dimech had taken over, and was going through it all again with Danny, right now, point by point.

The hot morning sun was casting half the street in umber shadow, and the women of Valletta were out with their shopping baskets, trailing children. Borg set off back to headquarters.

If Danny did it, he thought, he'll fight every inch of the way. It'll be like drawing teeth to get a confession. We've still got capital punishment in Malta, though it hasn't been invoked since heaven knows when. But the Maltese won't wear a child-murder—he's been here long enough to know *that*!

A holiday community exists in a limbo of largely meaningless self-indulgence compounded of eating and drinking, working hard on the progress of The Tan, looking for a new love-affair (or trying to find a new basis for the old), making sure the kids get well set-up for next winter, getting your money's worth.

With the news of the tragedy, the pattern changed at the Sunshine Hotel. After breakfast that day, the beach was deserted. Instead, they crowded the terrace in deckchairs, and sat in groups round tables in the lobby. The children were sent to play in the sandpits behind the hotel, out of sight. The place had the tone of a disaster area, or—more nearly—an area adjacent to a disaster: the valley next to the one where the dam has burst its wall. Someone remarked it was like the days of the London blitz all over again. Strangers who never spoke together on the beach shared tables; ill-assorted groupings with only vicarious horror in common: middle-aged couples and lovers of one night, huddled together in breathless speculation.

'Do you think they'll ever find the little lad's body?'

'It's the waiting that's so unbearable. We were to have gone to Valletta this morning, you know. But I had to stay in case there was news.'

'Not to speak ill of the dead, but that girl was just the sort to get herself done in. I was only saying so the other day, wasn't I, Stan?'

'My heart bleeds for that poor father.'

'My hubby says it's different here. There's no tide like we have at home, see? Things don't get washed up in the Mediterranean.'

'The warships are all out. I saw them from my window early. Going very slowly, right out at sea, and flashing signals to each other.'

'Oh dear, I hope it won't come to the worst!'

'We can't dare to hope. Let me get you a brandy, Ma.'

The groups broke and re-formed; a constantly changing pattern with its centre on the red-eyed chit of a girl who sat huddled in a squabby leather armchair in the middle of the lobby, keening quietly to herself and screwing a knot of wet handkerchief between her nervous fingers: Henrietta Milner. And Richard Needham was perched on the edge of a coffee table beside her. From time to time he reached out to touch her hand.

'Don't you think it would be better if you flew home, Henrietta?' he said. 'I'll ring up and fix your flight booking.'

'I expect I should,' she whispered. 'But I shall never forget it as long as I live. It was awful!'

Needham looked round despairingly, and was relieved to see the gaunt figure of Major Marker striding towards them, carrying a glass.

'A pick-me-up for the little lady,' he said solicitously.

'You must let me pay,' said Needham, fumbling in his pocket.

'Won't hear of it, dear boy,' boomed Major Marker. 'We're all in this together, aren't we?'

Borg the manager watched from behind his counter. He was wearing a black tie, with the ends tucked into the front buttoning of his shirt: tired eyes flickering anxiously over the crowded lobby.

It was ten o'clock.

At ten past, a police car came to a halt outside the open plate-glass doors, under the awning. Detective Constable Mike Agius was at the wheel. He remained there, casually lit a cigarette, heedless of the regarding eyes, settling back in his seat with a muscular brown arm laid elegantly along the window ledge of the door.

A few minutes later, the lift doors slid open, and the eyes panned to Mark Rattigan, who got out with Deborah Tarrant. She was wearing dark glasses. She made a tentative move to take his elbow, but her hand fell away irresolutely. Rattigan walked swiftly, with his stick probing delicately before his feet. They crossed the lobby through a pall of silence. Agius reached back and opened the passenger door, and they got in. The car slid out of sight.

The hubbub began again.

'Do you think they're been summoned because? . . . well . . .'

'That young woman appears to have insinuated herself into the nucleus of the situation!' The bass blare of Mrs Major Marker.

'It was horrible! I can't *begin* to tell you how horrible it was,' said Henrietta Milner plaintively, regaining lost ground.

They gathered round her again . . .

'Inspector Borg thought you'd be best away from the folks in the hotel. Somewhere quiet,' said Mike Agius.

'Yes. He explained on the phone,' said Deborah. 'It's very kind of him.'

They were climbing the rutted, winding road up a steep escarpment to the Victoria Lines—the rock-hewn chain of fortifications that look down over the northwestern tip of Malta and shield the teeming towns behind. The windows were open, but the hot breath of the air brought no coolness to the damp skin.

'Where is this place?' asked Deborah. 'Birze . . .'

'Birzebbugia,' said Agius. 'It's a resort at the other end of the island, on the Marsaxlokk. Borg's aunt keeps a restaurant there. It's a quiet place. Homely. She'll give you good meals and look after you. And we'll be able to phone through to you there if . . . if there's any news.'

'Yes.' She stole a glance to Mark Rattigan. His expressionless blind eyes stared out at the sun-whitened crags, and his hands were steady on the crook of the walking stick.

They dipped down a shining black road shaded with dusty palms, and out into the sunlight of a village street, joining a queue of cheerfully impatient traffic—the brightly painted buses; smoky lorries plastered with transfer flowers and incongruous names: *St Teresa, Go-man-Go, Rockabilly Baby, Immaculate Conception, Manchester United*—all of them in a hurry to get somewhere, as if today were just like any other day, and death only existed in the dry earth of the graveyards along the way, where gaunt cypresses kept watch over the rusty wrought-iron crosses and the eternelles.

In silence, they skirted the complex of inlets radiating from the high-walled bulk of the citadel of Valletta: forests of yachts' masts in Msida and Pieta; Marsa, with the immensity of Grand Harbour as a backdrop. Beyond Tarxien it was countryside again: a two-lane highway sliced between the fields of tomatoes and sweet corn. A bare-legged urchin waved to them from his perch on the top of a well; a blindfolded donkey plodded a trodden circle round him, and the water wheel turned.

They topped a rise and saw the sea again; the hooked fingers of a wide bay; naked-looking oil storage tanks and anchored toy ships streaked to waterlines with rust.

'That's Marsaxlokk,' said Agius. 'Soon be there.'

The restaurant was a rambling, paint-flaked Victorian building at the end of a quiet road. Agius led the way through a squeaky swing door, and they were in a tall room with whitewashed walls and a chequered-tiled floor scrubbed pale. It smelt of new bread and basil. The breeze from the bay blew coolly through French windows that let out on to a shaded balcony with wrought-iron railings, and they saw the blinding, diamond surface of the water beyond.

'Good morning, sir. Hello again, Miss Tarrant!' She busied her way from behind the bar at the end of the room: a stout little woman in a rose-printed apron over a black dress. After a brief moment of confusion, Deborah recognised her as one of the ubiquitous aunts from the christening party: the mother of Manoel who had cut his hand. She was framing an enquiry about the boy when Agius grated something in Maltese, and the little woman replied, shaking her head sadly.

'There's no news,' said Agius. 'The Inspector phoned Mrs Spindoe just now to say there was no news.'

'It's a terrible thing. Terrible,' said Mrs Spindoe, touching Deborah's hands. And to Rattigan: 'Come and sit down in the cool of the balcony, sir.'

'I'll be getting back,' said Agius. His shy eyes lingered with Deborah. 'Are you sure you'll be okay?' And when she nodded gravely, he gave a small, ducking bow and elbowed his way through the swing door and out into the sunlight.

Mrs Spindoe ushered them through the French windows on to the balcony, pointing up to a faded photograph over the door: a square-bearded man in a naval cap set at a jaunty angle.

'My late husband,' she said. 'The late Chief Petty Officer Wilfred Spindoe, Royal Navy, and father of Manoel. He was a very fine gentleman, and he surely went straight to Heaven. Would you like some coffee—or perhaps something stronger?'

The shrieks of two boys at play amongst the rock pools beneath the balcony: naked, thin limbs burnt near-black and pearled with water droplets as they clambered out and stood jauntily staring up at the couple sipping coffee on the shaded balcony.

'Hey, mister! You going to chuck a penny for us then?'

Deborah took a coin from her bag, and watched it spin a bright arc, strike the water and go slanting down into the clear blueness. The small, dark forms slid after it. There was a scrimmage underwater—she could almost hear their joshing laughter—and the coin vanished in a thin hand.

'How old are they?' asked Rattigan.

'About nine or ten . . . older than Alec,' she said.

His forefinger traced the rim of his cup.

'Do you know?' he said. 'For six years . . . and until yesterday morning, when they brought me the news . . . *I've hated my son and wished he had never lived!*'

The chief was of the opinion they couldn't hold Danny on the evidence they had; but, with the search for the boy's body going on—and the likelihood of it being found at any time—he said Dimech could go through the statement with him once more, but the big Englishman would have to be sent on his way at midday.

Joe Borg was with the chief when Bonnici came in.

'Regarding Jennifer Kearley . . .'

'Any luck?' asked Borg.

'No one of that name's set foot on Malta this year,' said Bonnici. 'Not legally, at any rate.'

'Illegally?' grated the chief.

'You mean just stepped ashore from a yacht, sir? I've been on to the harbour boys, and Customs. They don't think so.'

'What about London?'

'Snap answer is they haven't a Jennifer Kearley on their missing persons file. But they're going to dig deeper and wire back.'

The chief's big chair squeaked protestingly as he leaned back and stared up at the ceiling, hands locked behind his head.

'So the little boy's personal dead body remains a fantasy,' he said.

'Sure. But that still leaves us with her watch,' said Borg.

They had married, he told Deborah, in May. And Annette had been radiant in a dress of wild white silk, decorated on the bodice and sleeves with white flowers, carrying a bouquet of white freesias and orchids. He knew this because they'd told him, and someone had read it aloud from the local newspaper's report, which was why he could deliver it pat.

Only, of course, he was already nearly blind by then; and Annette had been no more than one white shape amidst all the wavering dark shadows. But he'd never forget the touch of wild white silk while he lived.

Perhaps she cried. Do girls often cry at their weddings? Yes, he supposed they often did—even when they were marrying whole men. Poor Annette.

Honeymoon in Amalfi: up the winding cliff road out of the town, in a villa that looked out over the sea from a great height; a blueness so intense that it imprinted itself even on his own dying retina.

Annette had been his eyes. She had described the old women who laboured, each day, down the steep steps cut in the mountainside; down from the citrus groves, with the tops of the great baskets canted high above their stooping shoulders. The country people were so poor. There had been the delight of clambering hand in hand together down the terraced gardens of the villa—to the lowest level fifty feet above the surf—to pick lemons for breakfast fresh from the trees. He remembered the feel of their pock-marked, waxy roundness; the sharp scent of them on Annette's fingers when she touched his cheeks. But then they realised that collecting and selling the lemons was the perk of the old gardener employed by the agency who rented the villa—and they felt like rich thieves. Sitting, after dinner, on the little iron balcony, Annette had explained the reason for the voices that carried so clearly from out in the bay. He had almost seen the still sardine boats with the gas lamps lowered close to the water; a thousand pinpoints of light reaching halfway to Salerno.

'I think she cried then,' he said. 'I think she must have cried when she felt the words were inadequate to describe the lights of the boats down there in the bay, under the stars. Though I told her I could imagine it all very clearly.'

Deborah, who had been listening with mounting horror, could only nod dumbly.

'We were engaged for eighteen months,' he said. 'When we first met, I was only just beginning to have the eye trouble, and it hadn't been diagnosed as anything serious. Three months after we got back from our honeymoon, I was stone blind.

'Do you know, Miss Tarrant, I never offered her the chance to back out of her bargain? Was that bad? I could have said—couldn't I?—"Now, look here, Annette, there's no point in being all noble and dewy-eyed about this thing. If we walk out of that church door together, your arm will be guiding me, and it will go on being like that till death do us part. I'm the horse you bid for, sure; but the horse you bid for broke its leg on the way home from the sale, and he'll never carry anyone's colours past the winning post now."

'I talked myself into nearly saying something like that many times, but I couldn't face the thought of the darkness—not without her. And she never spoke of it. Never by so much as an inflection of her voice did she express that my blindness made any difference to our getting married.'

'You must both have been very much in love,' whispered Deborah. It sounded like a hollow condolence. Rattigan didn't reply.

A woman and a teenage girl came out on to the balcony. Identical straw hats and tow hair. They had to be mother and daughter: mother in a flowered print mini dress four inches above the pluckered fat of her knees; the girl bulging out of white shorts. Two pairs of green demon-queen sunglasses tinned on the couple in the shaded corner, and swung away.

The girl went over to the railing, posed there jangling the charm bracelet on her plump wrist, looking out across the water.

'It's a perfect day for yachting. Quite perfect,' the girl drawled in a loud, careful voice.

The mother had sat down, and was dabbing eau de cologne on her scarlet face.

'I wish you wouldn't go on, dear,' she said. 'If he'd wanted you to go, he'd have asked you, wouldn't he?'

'Mother!'

'Well, he didn't ask you, did he? I mean, he had plenty of chance. You hung around quite pointedly, and he took those other girls.'

'Mother . . . *please*!' The girl's dark glasses flashed towards Deborah, who looked down at her hands in sudden embarrassment.

The mother went on inexorably: 'Never mind, dear. There's another week to go, and you'll find plenty of nice boys to ask you out. We're enjoying ourselves, aren't we? The food's very good, and it's all very cultural. I mean, I think they *overdo* religion here, but the churches really are marvellous, there's no getting away from it.'

'I hate churches!' whispered the girl brokenly.

'What we'll do now,' said the mother, 'is to have a nice cool drink, then drive to see that Neolithic temple before lunch. And after lunch we'll go back to the hotel for a little nap. You know how tired you get in the afternoon with all this heat. It's the weight you carry. I was just the same at your age . . .'

'Hey . . . Phillipa!'

The shout came across the water, and a tan-coloured sail slid into sight from behind a row of moored boats.

'There's the yacht!' squealed the girl. 'I think he's coming to pick me up after all!'

It was a small sailboat, with the signs of a season's hiring written along its battered hull. It wallowed erratically, loaded down low in the water with four bikinied girls, and a youth who waved from the tiller.

'Want to come, Phillipa?'

'Coming!' screeched Phillipa. 'Mummy, I can go, can't I?' And without waiting for an answer, she ran.

Deborah watched the boat detachedly as it crabbed towards the rock pool beneath the balcony, its sail flapping. A lissom-limbed girl sat in the prow with her slender feet trailing in the water. The boat ground violently ten feet from the shore, keeling over. The girls screamed, and the boy saved himself by hanging on to the boom, which swung under his weight, spilling him into the bottom of the boat amongst the tangled, brown bodies of his companions.

'We nearly went over then!'

'Shipwreck! Women and children first!'

'Where's Phillipa? Come on, Phillipa, we can't stick here all day!'

The fat girl came in sight below, absurd in sequinned sandals as she teetered over the slippery rocks.

'Stupid! Take your shoes off. You'll have to paddle out to us!'

There was a splash. Deborah leapt to her feet and joined the mother at the railing. Phillipa was waist-deep in the water, scrabbling for the side of the boat, wailing.

'A leg and a wing! Up she comes!' Laughing, they dragged her up over the heeling side, quivering buttocks uppermost. The boat rocked perilously on to its opposite beam, and hung there.

'Let's go, then. Turn her round and take her out to sea, Paul,' shouted one of the girls.

The youth wrestled an oar from between the sprawling forms at the bottom of the boat, and lowered it over the side. He bore down against it; the boat rolled again, but stayed in the same spot.

Deborah saw the reason now. 'You're hooked up on your centre board,' she said.

The youth cupped his hand to his ear. 'Wha-a-a-at?'

'The young lady says you're hooked up on your *sender* board!' shrilled Phillipa's mother.

After an instant of bafflement, he gave a start of comprehension; elbowed his way on hands and knees to haul up the weighted slab of keel upon which they were perched. Unpinned from the rocky bottom, the overladen craft slewed round as a wayward gust of wind billowed the sail, carrying them before it, away through the moorings; slanting from side to side as the boy made wild swings with the tiller to avoid hitting the other boats; out into open water.

'It's nicer for her to be with young things her own age,' said Phillipa's mother complacently. 'She'll soon dry off in the sunshine. I always think yachting's so chic, don't you?'

The boat was two hundred yards away now, and heading for the middle of the bay. Nothing in front of it but grey gulls wheeling over a slab-sided oil tanker and the crawling lines of distant breakers beyond the wide-open arms of the low headlands. Three near-naked figures, the boy's pink shirt, the fat girl in the silly straw hat—bare inches above the water and riding to God knows where.

'They're going nicely now, aren't they?' said the woman.

Deborah realised that she was trembling uncontrollably, and Rattigan must have sensed it when she sat down, because he said: 'That seems to have upset you. Why?'

'They shouldn't go out there,' she said. 'Someone should fetch them back. But because the sun's shining, and they're young . . .' her voice rose shrilly, but she was past caring about the horrified stare of the fat woman's big black glasses . . . 'because it's all a big silly joke, and the sea's so bland and blue, no one gives a thought to how easily—how terribly easily—the sea can kill!'

The time was eleven forty-eight . . .

Seventeen miles southwest of Rabat cathedral dome—which was just a white dot in the grey haze of the distant island—the helicopter pilot turned to bring them on another leg of their search pattern, and as he did so he saw something dip in the trough of the low swell a hundred feet below. He tapped the shoulder of the crewman crouched by the open door, and stabbed a downward-pointing finger. The other plucked the peak of his baseball cap further over his eyebrows, against the glare, and focussed his binoculars.

'It's a body!' he shouted above the clatter of the rotor blades. *'It's him all right!'*

CHAPTER 10

Danny Harcourt had only just been released a couple of minutes earlier: when the phone message came through from Fort St Angelo, Agius ran after him and picked him up a block away.

They drove down to the harbour in a patrol car, Borg and Agius sitting with Danny in the back: under the strung lines of washing that spanned the steep streets of tenements, and through the massive stone archway on to the quay. Twenty yards of oil-slicked water separated them from a French cruise liner moored slantingly across the harbour: Gallic faces looking down from the taffrail, where a tricolour ruffled restlessly. The sky was like the inside of a polished brass bell, and there were mare's tails stretched like teased-out cotton wool low down to the west. Rain was on the way.

The Englishman was slumped like a big rag doll in the back seat, his eyes glazed with fear. They met Borg's questioningly as the two detectives got out.

'You just stay right where you are, Mr Harcourt,' growled Borg, and slammed the door.

The chief's Humber glided under the archway, and the uniformed driver made a big thing of leaping out to open his door, snapping to a salute.

'What's happening, Borg?' asked the chief.

The patrol launch is supposed to be on its way here now, sir,' said Borg. 'The helicopter saw them take the body aboard, and radioed that it was heading back to Valletta at full speed. Should be here within the next quarter of an hour.'

'With the boy's body?'

'Yes.'

The chief fidgetted. 'Walk up and down with me for a while, Borg.'

Twenty paces to the steps at the end of the quay; to and fro, with hands clasped behind their backs, shoulders hunched. Mike Agius and the uniformed men stood round the patrol car. And the shocked eyes of the man in the back seat never left the two walkers for an instant.

'And what about *him*?' said the chief. 'You're hoping that he'll crack?'

'I think he will,' said Borg. 'If he did it—yes—he'll crack now.'

'I still think you're assuming a hell of a lot from very little evidence. Have you informed the father yet?'

'No. I thought we'd get this thing over first. It isn't going to be very pleasant. I've arranged with the harbour master for the use of that shed over there . . .' Borg pointed . . . 'as a temporary mortuary, for the identification.'

'There won't be any question of the father making an identification, being blind. Anyone else? . . . Miss Tarrant?'

Borg shook his head. 'I think we should spare her from that. There'll be the hotel manager. I've sent for him to come.'

A motor boat made a sweeping curve round the liner's stem and stopped by the scrubbed white stairway leading down from the ship's deck. A file of passengers passed down and took their places in the boat: day trippers, with buses waiting beyond the quay to take them on a conducted tour of the island: Mosta dome and the Citta Notabile, the trashy souvenir shops of Kingsway, the catacombs, some bland white beach and—tonight—the honkeytonk dives of the Gut.

'Here comes the patrol launch!' shouted Agius, and they saw it come round the corner of the breakwater, bow wave creaming under its chine.

'Stop that boatload of tourists from landing here,' snapped the chief. 'We don't want them around when they bring the body ashore. Tell the boatman to go to another quay.'

This was done; and they waited and watched as the launch drew near. Borg registered that a vein was tapping out a message above the corner of his right eye; he wiped the palms of his damp hands on his trouser hips, and wished he were anywhere else on God's earth.

It was an army launch, with an R.A.S.C. sergeant as coxswain. He was young, and the salt rime from the spray was dried on his cheeks.

He jumped ashore and nodded curtly to Borg. 'It's all yours,' he said. 'Will your chaps lift the stretcher out? Mine have had a bellyful.'

Two constables climbed down into the well of the launch, under the canopy, and came up awkwardly juggling a stretcher between them. The jouncing moved the thing that lay shrouded under a sailcloth.

'She's been dead quite a while,' muttered the sergeant. 'Though there's no way of knowing how long, offhand, is there, in this heat?'

And when he met Borg's stupefied stare: 'It's not the boy, you know. Didn't they tell you? No, I suppose they didn't see it very clearly from the chopper . . . It's the body of a girl!'

Mrs Spindoe didn't consult them about lunch; merely laid a

crisp white cloth on the table between them, and served minute steaks with tomato salad and a bottle of local red wine. She stood, smiling and nodding encouragingly, waiting for them to begin, which they did—but only for her sake.

When Deborah was called to the phone, Mark Rattigan sat through the long silence, blind eyes closed, hands folded on the table before him. Touching the sun-warmed metal of a spoon, he picked it up and bent it between his fingers. When he heard the tap-tapping of her returning footsteps, he let it drop, and it fell with a tinny clatter to the tiled floor.

'They've found Alec,' he said dully.

'Not Alec. They've found the body of another girl right out at sea.'

Rattigan exhaled a shuddering breath and buried his face in his hands.

It isn't finished yet, she thought. It's got to go on to the awful end, this agonised waiting. And no hope. What can I do for him? What can I say? I stumbled into this thing by chance, and I'm involved—emotionally involved—because of the bond that suddenly appeared between Alec and me that afternoon in Valletta. But what *real* right have I to be sharing his agony?

She sat down. 'That was Inspector Borg. He asks us to take a taxi back to the hotel and meet him there at three o'clock. He wants me to go through everything again—everything I can remember about Alec in those few hours I knew him.'

Rattigan lowered his hands. His face was quite composed.

'Who's the girl—Jennifer Kearley?'

'I don't know,' said Deborah. 'He didn't say, but I suppose it must be.'

Silent-footed, Mrs Spindoe came out on to the balcony. There were tears on her plump, brown cheeks. She had stood by Deborah's elbow at the phone, and knew that Mark Rattigan's ordeal was not yet over. Her eyes were all compassion; there was compassion in her very fingertips as she quietly took their plates with the barely tasted food, and stole out.

'We'll sit for a little while if you like,' said Deborah. 'There's plenty of time. He won't be at the hotel till three.' Because, when we've left here, she thought, the phone might ring again. And next time it might be the ultimate horror. Somewhere in the taxi between here and the hotel—in the parched countryside, or in those teeming streets—we might live through that moment, all unknowing.

She glanced at Rattigan again, and then looked away—because she remembered what he'd said about blind people *knowing*: but a slanting ray of sunlight was casting the shadow of his profile on the wall, and she was able to watch that.

What was in his mind now?

Remorse, perhaps. For hating the child who had won life by destroying the woman he loved . . .

The chief had cancelled his fortnight's leave, and sent his wife and kids on ahead to Taormina, in the hope that he'd be able to join them when it was all over: it seemed a thin prospect, the way tilings stood at the moment.

It was baking hot, threatening rain, and the humidity lay in pre-packaged slabs about the crowded C.I.D. office. The entire staff had declared a voluntary moratorium on off-duty: the room was crowded with shirtsleeved men, and all talking at once.

Mike Agius—who should have turned out for a practice game with the Sirens that afternoon—had stayed to check over the typist's transcript of his notes. He elbowed his way past the crush and slipped the sheaf in front of Borg, who was sitting with the phone jammed under the angle of his jaw, a pencil poised in one hand and a can of lager in the other, waiting on the line to London.

Borg's eyes flickered down the top sheet:

SUMMARY

1. Body sighted by U. S. Navy helicopter in position given as 17m S.W. Rabat. Brought to Valletta in patrol launch M70 (Sgt. A. Villiers R.A.O.C.).

2. Body found to be of a well-nourished girl, aged 20–23, height 5'4", medium build, brown hair, brown eyes.

3. Identity of deceased suggested by Harcourt (quote: "I think her name's Davis or something. She stayed at the hotel. I haven't seen her for days, and I thought she'd gone home to England. I only saw her on the beach, and only exchanged a few casual words with her. I didn't even chat her up. You can't hang this one on me").

4. Identity of deceased confirmed by V. Borg the hotel manager (quote: "Her name's Miss Eileen Davis. She stayed at the hotel for two weeks, and checked out on Monday evening. Took a taxi to the airport to fly back to England. I simply can't understand it").

5. Examination of hotel register established deceased to be Eileen M. Davis of 17, Constance Terrace, London S.W.7. Letter dispatched on January 17 of this year to hotel to book single room confirms address, as does Immigration card. Deceased was unaccompanied.

6. Interim report from police surgeon gives cause of death as strangulation. Time of death: 4–5 days prior to discovery, immersed in sea 3–4 days prior to discovery. No evidence of sexual assault.

The phone crackled in Borg's ear. He held up his hand, and the chattering ceased. The tension in the overheated office slipped breathlessly into top gear.

'Hello, yes' . . . a long pause, and the tapping of Borg's pencil on the desk top sounded like a death watch beetle in a dying house . . . 'She didn't? . . . no one's made any enquiries? . . . okay, thanks . . . you'll work on it and ring me back? Thanks. Ciaou!' He quietly put down the receiver.

'Well?' asked Agius.

Borg ran his lean hand, wearily, across his damp face. 'She lived alone,' he said. 'A patrol car's round at her flat right now. The landlady lives on the premises, and was expecting her back earlier this week. She hadn't got around to being worried; knows practically nothing about the girl—whether she had any relatives or friends. But no one's raised a squawk about her being missing yet. Were still in square one. Will somebody give me a light, please?'

He got up carrying his jacket; took Agius by the elbow and guided him towards the door. It was quiet and cool in the stone vault of the corridor, and Borg's eyes went towards the plate glass doors of the chapel.

DOMINE DIRIGE NOS

'Look, Mike,' he said, 'the photo section's trying to get some decent portrait shots of the girl; something fit to be shown. Go and see if they're ready, and hand them out to the boys in there. I want them shown to every barman, beach boy and headwaiter on the islands. And I want to know who she was with, if she was with anybody. If it was a man, I want him identified. Got that?'

Agius nodded eagerly. 'You think it will be Harcourt?'

'He's still our best bet,' said Borg. 'Though he reacted almost with relief when he saw the girl's body. Like it was indeed someone with whom he'd only exchanged a few casual words on the beach. But we had to let him go; there's just nothing to hold him on any longer.' They walked out to Borg's car, which was standing in a patch of shade by the courtyard wall. There came the chattering of an aero engine, and a helicopter swept over their heads, its cast shadow scurrying like a giant black spider over the white walk of the houses.

'They're still searching,' said Agius.

'*Two* bodies now,' said Borg. 'The boy's and—now we know she's for real—Jennifer Kearley's. We're dealing with a mass-murderer, Mike.'

'Or the Mafia?'

'The whole thing's beginning to look more Mafia-sized, I'll grant you that,' replied Borg.

They left Mark Rattigan sitting in his room by the telephone, and went out together on to the terrace; past the swimming pool and beyond, to the rock-strewn scrub on the headland overlooking the end of the beach. Down below, the flecked, blue shadows were patterned with brown bodies and the bright colours of swimsuits, and the lines of deckchairs stretched back from the shore line to the refreshment kiosk. The initial shock of the tragedy in their midst was already softening round the edges, and life was returning to the holiday pattern for the hotel guests.

'Everything,' Borg was saying, 'everything you can remember, no matter how inconsequential. There's something missing; something I can't put my finger on. But I've a feeling you might hold the key to this thing. Let me have it all over again. Right from the moment you first met Alec on the beach.'

From where they were sitting—on a smooth slab of sand-stone near the cliff edge—Deborah could have thrown a stone to hit the spot, twenty yards along the beach from where the ski-boats were moored, where she had lain that morning and looked up into Alec's regarding eyes.

"*Hello*," he had said . . .

She repeated everything that had passed between them, word for word, as well as she could remember: her offer to take Alec to Valletta; the bus journey when he had nearly been sick; the incidents of the toy shop, waiting for him outside the urinal; her irritation in the armoury. She choked on a sob when she came to speak of the moment of agonised relief in the parched garden above Grand Harbour, when her arms had enfolded his skinny, dancing legs.

Borg's flecked eyes were soft with sympathy. 'And it was in the bus on the way back to the hotel that you made him promise to give the watch to Gloria?'

'Yes.'

'We don't know if he did, of course,' said Borg. 'And that could be important.'

'I'm sure he would have done,' she said.

'And you never saw him again after that, did you? His note that you gave to me: he said there that he had fish and chips for dinner, and was sorry he didn't see you in the restaurant.'

'I never saw him again,' she whispered. She looked away, shutting her eyes tightly; and then, with sudden vehemence: 'Who could have done it? What sort of animal could have killed those two girls—and a helpless little boy?'

'A maniac,' said Borg soberly. He studied her face to decide how much more she could take. 'Mike Agius has a fixation about it being the work of the Mafia, and that's not entirely out of the question. But I think the murderer is a madman. Possibly a sex maniac, perhaps not . . . is something the matter, Miss Tarrant? Why are you looking like that?'

Slack-mouthed, she was staring out across the beach, towards the tower on the far headland: warm-walled, now, and curiously inviting against the Mediterranean sky. Quite different from—that night.

She shuddered . . .

'You've remembered something else?' he prompted.

And then she told him how she had been followed that night, by the bird-creature; and how she had seen it again, on the frosted glass of the restaurant door. Horrified by the implications of what she was saying, nauseated by a sudden, stark image of her own corpse floating in the sea wrack, she faltered the name of the bird-creature.

'I'll see Major Marker right away,' said Borg quietly.

But the Markers had gone to Valletta, and were not expected back for dinner.

The clerk behind the reception desk at the Casino was from Zebbiegh and had been at school with Bonnici. He obligingly took out a thick bundle of admission counterfoils for the previous week and came up with a lucky, quick answer.

'Here we are, then, Carmel,' he said, passing over one of the books, 'Miss Eileen Davis. She was here last Saturday evening, you see.'

'You issue a personal ticket for every admission, don't you? I want to know if she was accompanied—and I'm really only interested if it was a man.'

The clerk flipped over the flimsy pages. 'The two before Miss Davis were a Mr F. Frost and a Mrs G. Frost . . . and the following . . . both of them ladies.'

'Not interested, Peter. Not right now, at any rate. I'd be interested in a chap named Daniel Harcourt.'

'Well, we have two admission books going at the same time,

three if it's a busy evening. Maybe if she was with someone they went to different clerks, to save time; there'd be a queue of three or four people at each clerk on a Saturday evening. Or again, she might have met this man inside.'

'I'd like you to check that for me, please, Peter.'

The clerk made a moue and tapped the pile of books. Tor you I'll do it, Carmel. It may take a few minutes.'

'I'll go and have a look inside while you're doing it,' said Bonnici.

The great columned hall was unlit, and the air conditioning met him with a tang of vanilla ice cream when he pushed open the glass doors. The Casino opened at eight; the gaming tables were still covered with white shrouds. There were lights coming from the bar, behind the colonnaded screen at the far end, and someone was whistling an Italian pop tune. He crossed the hall, under the humming fans.

A thick-set barman in shirtsleeves was polishing glasses, his black-pelted fingers probing as delicately as a woman's. He saw Bonnici's reflection in a mirror and did not bother to turn round.

'We're still closed.'

'Police,' said Bonnici. 'C.I.D.' He slipped the photograph across the counter. 'Have you seen this woman in here recently—like last Saturday, for instance?'

The man finished his glass; set it carefully on a shelf, positioning it with a fingertip. Then he laboriously took out a pair of steel-rimmed glasses, set them low on his broad nose, and picked up the photograph.

'Dead, is she?'

'Well dead,' said Bonnici wearily.

'You can always tell. It's the eyes.'

'Yes. Do you remember her?'

'Harry!' bawled the barman. A door at the far end of the bar bounced open and a pale-faced youth struggled in carrying a crate of beer. 'Take a look at this picture, Harry. It's the police.'

Harry nodded over the print, a long cowlick of black hair flopping.

'Have you seen her in here?' asked Bonnici.

'Oh, yes. She was here Saturday. She sat over there, at the table in the corner, by the door. I served her.'

'Alone?'

'Yes. At first. Then this man at the bar told me to take her the same again, with his compliments. She looked a bit surprised, but he waved to her from the bar, as if he knew her, and she smiled back. Then he went over and sat with her.'

Bonnici was suddenly aware of a pulse throbbing in his temple.

'Could you describe this man?' he asked.

The clerk met Bonnici halfway across the hall. He was grinning smugly and carrying an open book of counterfoils.

'I've found your chap you're looking for!'

'We've both found him,' said Bonnici. 'And now I'd like to use your telephone, Peter.'

A few minutes later, he was connected with Borg at the hotel.

'Good work, Bonnici,' said Borg. 'Get over to St Paul's right away. I'll have a squad car meet you at Harcourt's flat. They'll take him in and leave one man with you. He'll help you go through the place. I want it torn apart from top to bottom. Got that?'

'For what?'

'For the watch marked Jennifer Kearley . . . and anything else you can find!'

Telex from New Scotland Yard, addressed to C.I.D. Valletta, timed at 1720 hours C.E.T.:

Reference Eileen Davis. Enquiries establish that her mother Mrs

> *Jennifer Davis, nee Kearley, died of natural causes 18.2.67. Wristwatch presumably a legacy to daughter . . .*

So it was out, now. The secret fantasy of Alec Hugo Rattigan had been no fantasy. The dead lady of his very own had been Eileen Davis, the well-nourished, medium-built girl from Flat 18; 17, Constance Terrace, S.W.7. But she had not smelt at that time.

CHAPTER 11

By five forty-five, the September day bowed to the oppressive authority of the *sirocco* and gave up hying. The first rain fell over the southeastern part of the main island, and advanced to cover it from Marsaxlokk to Gozo.

In Queen's Square in Valletta, where they sat at table with their ices and coffee and frosted beer, the downpour sent them swarming for shelter with sodden newspapers over their heads.

In a hundred towns and villages lying beneath the high domes of churches, the dogs on the flat rooftops cowered and whined to the roar of the gutters cascading into the narrow streets and the secret courtyards of walled houses.

Out on the stark hillsides, water streamed over pitted rocks and into the shallow valleys, bringing down the red ooze of the sparse Maltese earth; and the churning lorry wheels carried it from country lanes and plastered it in terra cotta streaks along the highways.

A traffic cop stood with rain rebounding knee-high all round him, and squinted out into the gloom, to the wavering headlights, lost in a world of sudden water.

A black crocodile of boy seminarists, trapped at the limit of their afternoon walk, raced back on the heels of their high-stepping tutor; whooping with release and stamping in the deep puddles.

In a drenched graveyard, huddled round a naked pit under the cypresses, a party of mourners watched the muddy water rise around the coffin and the rain hammer upon its lid, while the soaked priest intoned.

When the overcast came lower to meet the sea, the searching helicopters dipped down with it; slicing above the waves, with the crews peering through their streaming canopies. Down at sea level, grey met grey in a waste of nothingness; blinding the men on the minesweepers' open bridges.

At a few minutes to six, the signal went out to call off the search for the boy's body, because of adverse weather conditions.

They sat together near the open French windows of Mark Rattigan's hotel room with the rain sluicing down on to the tiled balcony outside; beyond that, the beach and the headland.

The lights were on in the room, and she felt unaccountably warm and protected. The rhododendron-lined road and the dark tower were a whole world away, and the disquietening image of the bird-creature—now it was shared with Borg—was just an image.

Two detectives were waiting down in the hall for the Markers to return; but that was something to come—either a horror or an embarrassment—which she crammed out of her mind. Meanwhile, Borg had gone back to headquarters to deal with something that had just turned up: some new development concerning the girl they'd found this morning, he'd said.

So now there was only the waiting; the waiting and the sharing. She'd done most of the talking in the last hour: had told him all about Diana, the house at South-wold, the coffee matrons, and Icarus' silver wings hanging from the ceiling of the museum in Kennington. But she'd jibbed at speaking of the white-skinned boy with the clip-on bow tie. And now a silence lay between them like a winding sheet.

'What shall you do now, then—when you get back to England?'

His voice—sudden and loud above the noise of the rain—made her start. Did he really want to know? Was he really interested in Deborah Tarrant? No. It was all part of the elaborate charade they were acting out together, to shut out the agony of waiting.

'I think I shall move to London and take a job,' she said, after a few moments' reflection. 'Sell up the house and make a start on my own.'

'Perhaps you'll marry quite soon,' he said. 'I think you seem to be the sort of person who needs people. From what I gather, you even needed your mother. All those years . . . your complete subservience to her . . . you'll find life empty after that. Prisoners leap to lose their chains, but the world outside prison walls can be a frightening place.' He took out a cigarette and a match, laying them side by side between his fingers, and striking the match so that the flame charred the end of the cigarette and he was able to draw it to life between his lips. 'Yes, I think you'll have to be very careful about that. Six months alone in London—and London's one place on earth, above all others, where you can be bone and skeleton without anyone giving a damn—and you could rush into a relationship with a substitute mother-figure, and be right back where you started. But there isn't any alternative for you, is there? You're obviously not promiscuous, nor find it easy to make casual relationships.'

She flushed. 'How can you know that?'

'On your own evidence. You spent one morning on a crowded beach in Malta, wearing a bikini. Young and—I presume—attractive to look at. What happened? You struck up a friendship with a six-year-old boy. I haven't offended you?'

'No.' She smiled. 'You're quite right. I am rather like a freed prisoner. It all seems strangely frightening, and I shrink away from the new and difficult things. Like people . . . men.'

'But you're strong, for all that,' he said. 'Your basic strength has been . . . is being . . . a great help to me. And I'm grateful. All in all, this hasn't turned out to be a very pleasant holiday for you.' He exhaled a cloud of smoke, and she watched it drift out of the window, to be dissipated by the rain. 'And it promises to be a hell of a lot less pleasant,' he added flatly.

She struggled to form phrases in her mind: word images to make contact with him, the hand stretched out across the darkness. And when they were assembled, she began tentatively: 'You were talking about loneliness . . .'

'Yes?'

'I can't begin to tell you what it was like, the day of Diana's inquest,' she said. 'They were all terribly nice to me in that stuffy little room. The coroner whose wife was one of Diana's coffee friends; the police inspector who'd taken my hand and led me across the road when I was a little girl and he a constable. They were all so kind. Accidental Death, and the court's deepest sympathy to Miss Tarrant, who should consider herself in no way responsible for her mother's tragic end. I walked back to the house, and I was completely anaesthetised: no emotions whatever, completely drained. It wasn't till I shut the front door behind me, and looked down the gloomy hallway—towards the oval-topped window at the far end, with a view of the sea—that it began: the feeling of loss, the panic-stricken sense of aloneness in an alien world. Then there was Diana's cardigan hanging on the peg by the garden door, and the floppy-brimmed straw hat she wore when she tended her roses. I trembled when I saw them; touched them, and tried to draw something from them; something of Diana's vitality which had dominated my life, which I'd feared and resented—but had learned to lean on . . .'

No sound but the slashing of the rain. She glanced at him covertly; his head was bowed.

(Doesn't he realise? It was quite different for him, because he loved Annette, but this *must* tell him that I can go halfway towards understanding how he must have felt when he lost her!)

'Yes,' he said. 'You're quite right. The sense of being bereft: that's what starts up the panic in the heart. I know what you mean.'

(Talk to me about it! Say it! Tell me how you felt when you went from that nursing home; leaving your Annette behind you, with the screaming fragment of new life that you must have hated and resented so. Talk! Cry if you want to! Only don't just sit there and destroy yourself with remorse.)

'We become conditioned to relying on another person,' he said. 'You and your mother; I and Annette.'

'Yes.' Eagerly.

'Love,' he said. 'Love hardly matters. *Hate* is just as potent—as a conditioner.'

And when she stared at him, suddenly appalled: 'I appreciate what you're trying to do, Miss Tarrant . . . or may I call you Deborah? . . .' there was an edge of wry mockery in his voice . . . 'but at the risk of destroying your very tender and kindly reaction to a blind widower with a murdered son, I should tell you. . . .'

He got to his feet, fumbling his white-painted stick and cursing softly when he picked it up. Deborah realised that he had been drinking—alone—while she had been with Borg. He lurched two paces towards the windows, and leaned there. She saw spray from the rain dappling his face.

'I drank nearly all of a bottle of whisky when I got home that night,' he said. 'That was before the sense of being bereft set in. My first reaction was one of blessed relief.' He turned towards her. 'My wife had shown herself to be a whore, you see, Deborah!

'A whore . . . God rest her soul!'

Borg came down from the canteen with Mike Agius. There was an uncomfortable feeling under his belt. Not having eaten all day, he had waded—with soulless detachment—through a large portion of macaroni cheese, his favourite dish; firing questions at Agius all the time, testing his reactions, scribbling notes. He decided he felt terrible.

He rapped on the office door, and Detective Sergeant Camilleri came out. He saw Danny Harcourt sitting inside there, facing Detective Constable Vella, and the blond Englishman was looking pretty quenched. The door swung to.

'Any joy, then?'

'He's all yours,' said Camilleri. Camilleri was carrying his jacket, and the sweat radiated in two circular dark patches from the armpits of his shirt. He wiped a forearm across his homely, pugilist's face. 'I can't get anywhere with him. Mother of God, but I've tried.'

Borg nodded and opened the door. A signal with his eyes brought Vella to his feet.

'Goodnight, Inspector Borg.'

'Goodnight, Vella.'

Mike Agius took Vella's seat. Borg slid out a cigarette and tossed the packet to his assistant. Snapping his lighter, he lowered himself deliberately into his chair and opened a drawer. Bringing out a sheaf of foolscap typescript, he swung back in the chair, luxuriantly exhaling.

'Now, you know, Detective Constable Agius,' he said

ponderously, 'I think you have something here. This Mafia report of yours. Yes, I like it.'

'Thank you, Inspector,' murmured Agius, primly.

'Here's what I like about it,' said Borg. 'It's got what I call pristine simplicity and conviction.'

Agius smirked.

'Let's examine your premises, then. To start with, you suppose a Mafia drug ring right here in Valletta. This makes sense. Heaven knows how many private craft nose in and out of Malta in every twenty-four hours—and how many of them come from Tunisia, Egypt, the Levant?'

'With Sicily the next stop,' supplied Agius, cocking an eye towards the blond Englishman, who sat looking at his hands. 'Or direct to the Italian mainland, bypassing the anti-narcotic patrols concentrated round Sicily . . .'

'Then straight to the markets of Europe,' said Borg. 'The cafés and bars of the Kings Road, the Boulevard St Michel, Kurfürstendamm and Rembrandtsplein; for the hop-headed kids who're the cash customers. Yes, I like it, Agius. The raw material from North Africa and the Levant, brought here in small quantities; Malta used as a clearing house after the stuff's refined; then onward transmission to Europe. And I'll tell you another possibility you never mentioned in your report . . .'

'What's that, sir?' Agius was still watching Harcourt.

'The possibility of them using homeward-bound tourists as carriers,' said Borg. 'Not in a big way, of course. The old and tried method of bulk-carrying—by crew members of ships and aircraft who do it on a regular, professional basis, and know all the angles—is safest and best. But there'd be an opening for a keen middle man who could persuade say, half a dozen respectable British fathers-of-family to earn fivers by posting packets of silk stockings to a girlfriend in London when they got home.'

'Or half a dozen young birds,' said Agius. 'If your middle man was a bit of a hand with the ladies, it would be a pushover for him. Particularly if this chap had the right contacts—social contacts, I mean.'

'Like a barman, or a waiter . . . a job where a good-looking chap with a smooth line of chat could do a bit of counter-jumping and romance the lady customers on more or less equal terms, if he had the cheek.'

'Beach boy would be better,' said Agius slowly. 'Swimming trunks iron out social differences. I've seen husky young village lads, who never wore shoes before they left school, snatch smashing birds from under the noses of narrow-chested yacht owners. Yes, Inspector, I think this middle man of yours would work on a beach, as either a beach boy . . . or . . .'

'NO!' Danny Harcourt's voice cracked at the top end of its register. Agius reached out and gently lowered him back to the seat.

'You . . . you can't do this to me! It wasn't like that at all!'

Joe Borg took out his wallet and extracted a folded envelope. He leaned forward and tipped the contents of the envelope on to the sheaf of typescript in the middle of the desk: a tablespoonful of white crystals, glistening like caster sugar.

The flecked eyes were as cold as a lizard's. 'One of our officers dug this out from behind the plaster of your ceiling less than an hour ago, Harcourt,' he said. 'So, if it wasn't like that, just you tell me how it was!' And then, holding the other's horrified gaze: 'We're going to nail this on you, Harcourt, if we have to ask Scotland Yard to interrogate every girl you ever entertained in that cosy top floor room of yours at the hotel.

'So, let's cut out the non essentials for the moment, Harcourt. You're in this drug ring, and I think we can prove it. You almost certainly killed Gloria Pritchard and Eileen Davis because they somehow found out about your game. Proving that can wait, too.

'What you're going to tell me now, right away, is at which part of the coast you dumped the body of that little lad!'

From Amalfi in May, to Kensington in June, with the scent of apple blossom in the tiny garden behind Church Street . . .

(And how he had loved her then, he told Deborah.)

Her face, her body, had been the last dear things ever to be imprinted behind his dying eyes; they still remained imprinted there in perfection; all he had to do was to reach out and renew the shapes with his fingertips. Stemming from the feel of her was his delight in everything else in life: the cool roundness of fruit, coarse-woven cloth, the plasticity of water, yielding sand; the whole tactile world had a new meaningfulness because Annette was his to touch.

And her voice. She indulged him recklessly with her voice: through it he saw the changing seasons in their private, walled garden, and in the streets where they walked hand in hand; and when there was nothing else to tell, she read to him—the newspapers, a book a week, his law journals, everything that came through the letterbox of their pink-painted door; and in the darkness of night, when they lay together and were both blind, there was still her voice close against his cheek.

Winter passed, and another new spring. Mondays to Fridays she drove him every morning to the University. At the end of the day, unless they were going out—in which case she picked him up—he took a taxi home, and she would be waiting at the open door: arms wound tightly about his neck; the clinging, yielding feel of her.

The day it all began to die was the Saturday May Davenport rang. Annette answered the phone and hissed Horrors, horrors, for God's sake throw me a quick excuse, darling. But he took the receiver from her. Come round, May, I've heard such a lot about you, and Annette never sees anyone but me nowadays.

May Davenport was fashion editor on one of the Evangeline Press women's glossies; Annette had modelled for them in the old days—the old days a year ago. May sounded tall, blue-rinsed and diamond-brittle. They had drinks in the garden, and he listened to them, nursing a quiet delight at the way Annette was obviously relishing the esoteric in-talk about press-dates, blow-ups, booms, paste-ups, such-and-such a model's newest guards' officer and the scandalous price of tulle.

(My Annette, I never knew there was so much of your life hidden from me . . .)

It was easy—because of Annette's delight—to feel indulgent towards May Davenport. It was he who stoutly supported the notion that darling Netty really should get out and about, don't you think? All that professional experience and that God-given beauty thrown away, and after all it's only been a year, she's still a face and a name.

Annette pleaded that she had everything she wanted right here, but they'd have none of it. In the end, May Davenport made a booking for her on the following Tuesday at Richard Norman's studio.

And when they were alone again, Now look what you've let me in for: ruefully, between kisses. But he told her it would make him happy to think that she had a life which extended beyond Church Street, the garden, the kitchen and him. She accepted this, because she sang in the car on Tuesday morning.

One booking a week. Soon she was describing the pictures to him, while he ran his fingers over the glossy magazine covers, imagining the familiar shape of her face smiling up at him. The phone rang more often. Indulgent, still, he grew used to taking messages: Tell Netty tomorrow's off, switched to the same time Friday, okay? Some of them had them both in stitches: We're doing a backless number and don't want strap marks, so tell Netty to skip her bra. The whole thing snowballed almost without them noticing it. By autumn, she was working every day. It became a good idea to have a daily woman who was willing to stay and fix supper—which he sometimes ate alone.

Paris seemed a good idea too. He would have gone with her, but was already fixed for a seminar at the University of Wessex. In the event, she went with May Davenport and Richard Ventris the photographer. Back from Wessex, he spent four desolate days at the house. There was a picture of Annette in the *Courier*, wearing a wedding dress from one of the collections; Mrs Sharp the daily woman described it to him.

Alone in the darkened sitting room, and then her key in the latch; yielding and soft as always, she was in his arms. Lying together that night, she murmured the story of how it had been in Paris: brilliant but terribly wearisome, but May had been fun, and Richard was a pet.

Soon after, they went to a party at Richard Ventris's studio: a cacophony of assured voices; unfamiliar scents; a vast room of baffling shape, with spidery contraptions of metal he kept stumbling into. He was introduced to a girl named Suzanne something who found them wicker chairs on an iron balcony, in the coolness. Suzanne something was in P.R., and appeared to think he'd come to the party on his own. He let her conversation pour over him like warm maple syrup, and ached for Annette.

Where's Netty? Richard's showing her his dark room, darling. Ha, ha. My dear, how long's it been going on? Darling, from Day One naturally. You know Richard . . . every day, and in every way, ha, ha.

Suzanne something was checked in mid-spate by the sound

of their voices (one of them was May Davenport's) drifting out through the French windows, then she giggled and carried on. He sat gripping the arms of the chair till his heart stopped hammering enough to allow him to draw breath. And then he screamed inside.

When Annette found him again, her hand was moist and feverish—like her voice—and he wiped his own palm clean, surreptitiously, against the lining of his pocket. They went home soon afterwards; in the taxi she was all vivacity, teetering on the verge of hysteria.

What of it? He put it to himself, with her sleeping, scented head on his bare shoulder; fought with the question all night, and came up with the only answer: I can bear it, for the sake of what she is to me; this is something she needs; this is something I can give back to her.

After that came the subterfuges: location jobs out of town, and one foggy night she phoned him to say she was stopping over at May's. Then there was the night he knew for certain that she was with Ventris, because of the laughter in her voice, and because she was wearing a new suit she hadn't told him about—his fingertips discovered the unfamiliar texture of the material. Before Mrs Sharp left him to his supper, he asked her to bring him a bottle of whisky from the off-license, and he was halfway down the bottle when the phone rang. He was in the middle of a self-destroying fantasy about the two of them together: touching and *seeing* each other. It was Ventris who seemed surprised at his surprise, and would he tell Netty that the session was cancelled for Tuesday?

(That was almost the worst part—when I knew she'd moved on to someone else.)

It went on. And he was never far behind her. The tang of yet another man's shaving lotion on her cheek, new voices when he answered the phone: you can't keep much from a blind man. He followed the ups and downs of her affairs, and became familiar with the whole cycle of each. It usually began with a restless boredom; this was when the house was too small for her, and they went out together to dinner, a theatre, a party. When she'd found a new man, the house vibrated to her gaiety—only she wasn't often in. This was the time for lonely suppers, with whisky to try to quench the fantasies. He began to take a vicarious pleasure in the middle periods: this was when the current affair had become a gentle habit with her; when she thought, perhaps, she was in love. Then she carried an aura of self-regarding contentment; cosseted herself like a beautiful, well-fed cat. And mixed in with this was a half-tender, half-remorseful attitude to him that showed itself in indulgence. Let's not go out tonight, darling. I'll read to you. It's been so long. Where did we leave our handsome hero?

The last phase of all, when the cycles blended together so that the pattern was lost: this was when he knew that she had lost track of even pretending about love, and was going to bed with two or more men; with any man, perhaps, who put up a reasonable proposition.

(And then—she told me she was going to have a baby.)

Flippantly: Look at me—what you see here is a girl with a tender secret. Eating for two. Knit small garments. Do you have any twins in your family, darling?

It was easy to deceive her—as she had tried to deceive him. He just took her hands and pressed them against his blind eyes and said nothing, because it was too late to say anything that could possibly alter it.

She carried on working for a while, and then the phone calls—all the phone calls—tailed off to nothing. He took leave of absence and they went away together to the Lake District, where it rained all the while, and Annette sulked indoors with a book, while he sat alone in an arbour behind the hotel with the rain drumming on the roof, and nurtured his hatred with the thought of another man's bastard he was going to have to accept.

'When did you begin to hate her?' asked Deborah.

'If I ever hated her,' said Rattigan, 'if I still hate her now, it must have begun that night at the party, when she came to me after being with Ventris. Only, it developed gradually, and was more the slow dying of love than anything so positive as hatred. When she told me . . . about the baby . . . I deliberately stamped out the last spark of love. But that did nothing to stop my need for her. I never lost that need, right up to the end. And it's still the same. Just like you with your mother. We're both prisoners of need.'

'Alec's your child.'

'Yes.'

'That was how I recognised you at the airport.'

'If he weren't my son, but only Annette's, it wouldn't make any difference . . . not now . . . *I'd still want him back!*'

CHAPTER 12

Eight-thirty. Borg could only think of his older brother George, who held down a good job at the brewery, with a nice house in Hamrun, lovely wife and kids, and a beach chalet at Mellieha Bay; a forty-hour week, and no need to meet the eyes of dead girls nor trample about in the filth of other people's lives. And their mother thought that Joe had done best for himself: a police officer. Jesus!

Harcourt had been formally charged with possession of dangerous drugs and was in a cell. The rain had stopped, and the damp wind came in through the open office window, turning the place into a Turkish bath.

'Let's get some air, and chew over what we've got,' he said.

They walked in silence down the Mall, leaving Phoenicia Hotel on their left and crossing the grass island with the R.A.F. memorial column, towards the wall overlooking Grand Harbour.

The American fleet had left, and the surface of the water was oily-dark, with the full moon reflected as a perfect circle under the bastion of St Angelo.

They leaned against the wall, with the headlights of passing cars panning over them. Agius finished his cigarette and sent it spinning like a spent meteorite into the garden below. 'I thought we had him,' he said. 'It was like watching a fish in a net, hemmed in on all sides, so that all the flipping around in the world couldn't get it out. You played it a heat, and I thought we had him. With all that weight of evidence, how can he still be denying everything?'

'Fear perhaps,' said Borg. 'The long arm of the Mafia.'

'Omerta.'

Borg nodded. 'The code of silence. The Mafia's greatest weapon. You've never been to Sicily, have you, Mike? You can feel *omerta* all round you there, particularly in the mountain villages. Perhaps there'll be a little square with a church and a couple of bars—like in Qrendi or Zurrieq or a score of villages here in Malta—and you know that a chap was gunned to death on the cobblestones where you're standing, only the night before. You know, because you've seen the photos in the local nick, and they haven't made much of a job of cleaning away the bloodstains, either. And all the time, the men of the village are eyeing you from the doorways of the bars—only they look away when you try to meet their glance. And if you're with the local police inspector—I was at the time—you see the effect of his questioning. No effect! He's from the mainland, and not one of them; a man from outer space. He starts pretty optimistically: did anyone hear the shots? Anyone see it happen? Then, of course, because the murdered guy was a local, and—just like here in Malta—couldn't have turned over in bed without the whole village knowing, he asks if he had any enemies. That one gets the flattest stares of all.

'And then it dawns on you, Mike. This is *omerta* in living action. Not only have the men of the village washed their minds clean of the sound of gunshots, of the sight of the body lying in its own blood; they've made it so that the dead man never was, so that a murder never took place at all! And you wonder at Harcourt wriggling out of our net! He'll know what *omerta*'s all about if he's been handling drugs for the Mafia for any length of time.'

'But we've got him on the drugs charge,' said Agius. 'He denies that too, but his dabs were all over the plaster. How much more positive evidence before he admits it? How do we make him confess about the murders, and tell exactly where he dumped the boy's body overboard? I suppose he used one of his sailing boats.'

'Whoever committed the murders,' said Borg slowly, 'whether it was Harcourt or a person as yet unknown, almost certainly used one of the sailing boats, yes. It was done silently. At night.'

'Someone else?' said Agius, surprised. 'Like Marker, do you mean? Do you really think anyone else could have been implicated with those girls and the lad to the extent of murdering them, and no connection with Harcourt and the drug angle? That would be a hell of a coincidence, wouldn't it?'

A small coaster was coming into the harbour. Borg waited till its red and green navigation lights swung into view before he replied: 'Not all that much of a coincidence. By all accounts, Gloria Pritchard and Eileen Davis was physically the most attractive girls on the hotel beach at that time. Discounting his drug interests, Harcourt's a self-confessed womaniser, so it would be unlikely if he hadn't made a pass at the pair of them. Girls who look like that are in a constant state of being chatted-up. I've seen *you* at it, Mike.'

Agius grinned. 'You mean, if I'd been staying at the hotel, my beady eyes would have lit on those two girls, and I suppose you're right.'

'And what if you'd been the murderer? Not Harcourt. We'll have it for the moment that *you're* the murderer. Tell me what sort of man you are.'

'Mad,' said Agius gravely. 'What they call a psychopath, perhaps. Not the sort who'd go up to a pretty girl and date her; I'd leave that to fellows like Harcourt. Maybe the best I could do would be to have a few words with her at the bar, about the weather. But most of the time I'd just watch her, and follow her around. And that's why Inspector Borg of Valletta C.I.D. can't put his finger on me. Not unless my name's Marker.'

'Marker got a bit further than the weather,' said Borg. 'Not much further. But he did a certain amount of watching.'

'And following,' said Agius. 'I only saw Pritchard and Davis dead, but surely Miss Tarrant's in their physical class, and a lady with it.'

Borg lit another cigarette, and found to his surprise that his hand was trembling . . .

'Let's try another tack, Mike. Let's go back to Eileen Davis, who was the first to die. According to medical evidence, she was killed some time on Monday evening, and her body dumped into the sea about twenty-four hours later. At some time during that twenty-four hours, little Alec found the body and played Let's Pretend that it was his. What we've never really gone into is, where did he find her?'

'Harcourt's boathouse on the beach,' said Agius firmly. 'If Harcourt's our man it's the ready-made spot. There's a lot of expensive portable gear in there, outboard engines, nylon sails and the like, and he keeps it locked—even against the local lads who help him for cigarette money. But a nosy little beggar like Alec could have slipped in while the door was temporarily unlocked and Harcourt wasn't looking. That's what we've always assumed, isn't it?'

'Yes. But I grow to like it less. And what if Harcourt isn't our man—where then, Mike?'

* * *

Hot, restless and tense, she went out to look for coolness and solitude; somewhere to think. She left Mark Rattigan sitting by the window, staring blindly out into the night. They hadn't spoken for half an hour.

She came out of the lift into the arms of the stout woman who'd made the fuss about the lizard in the restaurant. The woman giggled the beginning of an apology, then did a myopic double take from behind her rimless glasses.

'Oh, it's *you*, my dear! Oh, I've felt so dreadful all this day, and I haven't seen you anywhere. Tell me, is there any news yet about . . . you know?'

Deborah shook her head and brushed past her. Borg the manager was hunched over the hotel register at the counter; his guilt-ridden eyes tried desperately to hold hers, seeking forgiveness. The two detectives were waiting for the Markers' return just inside the glass door on to the terrace. Big men with big brown shoes. They looked up when she passed them, then went back to their newspapers and mineral water.

The long row of dwarf burning bushes on the seaward edge of the terrace stood out starkly under the overhead lights, and were reflected in the deep puddles of rainwater that patterned the flagstones. Dinner was nearly over, and a few guests were drinking at tables against the white, stuccoed wall. Down at the far end of the terrace, beyond the loom of the lights, some children were playing hopscotch amongst the puddles. Deborah saw an empty table at the end, well away from the others, and made for it. No one took any notice of her. There had been a fresh influx of guests during the day. Most of the people on the terrace had the fish-belly whiteness of home, and she was a stranger to them.

She sat down, facing the darkness . . .

His basic decency, she decided, was reflected in that hideous story.

He had loved Annette as a whole man, and not merely because of his blind man's need for her. The need—and her response—had added gratitude to love. And when he failed with her it was only because of compassion: the compassion of a large heart that understood another person's frailty, and was ready to come to terms with it.

("Worried sick about money" . . . oh, Diana, would things have turned out differently if I'd ever felt any compassion for *your* weaknesses?)

No. Beware of compassion. It led Mark Rattigan to condone his wife's first act of faithlessness, out of gratitude. A giving-back, he'd said: something he could bear, for the sake of what she'd been—what she still was at that time—to him.

Only, he hadn't guessed how much he'd be called upon to give. And if he'd grown to hate her, it was only because he's an ordinary, mortal man who bleeds—and not a saint.

'Anybody's seats, love?'

Startled she turned her head. They were an elderly couple: grey, faceless people straight from England. While she'd been thinking, the tables on the terrace had all filled up.

'No. I'm on my own. Please do.'

'Sit you down, Mabel.'

The children's voices rose shrilly, and a barefoot boy in shorts and sweatshirt cannoned into the back of her chair and scrabbled for a bouncing ball. He carried it back to his friends, laughing.

Alec's face came back to Deborah, with a new and shuddering sense of deprivation.

'Time them kids was in bed,' said the woman, looking to Deborah for a nod of agreement. 'They wouldn't be allowed up this time at home, I'm sure.'

'It's travelling abroad as does it,' said her husband. 'What can you expect? Remember at Sitges last year? Them Spanish kids at the next table? All pasty-faced and black circles under their eyes, and falling asleep over their dinners at gone ten o'clock. Disgusting way to bring up kids. Our lot are at it now. That's foreign travel for you. Another couple of generations, and we'll *all* be foreigners!'

'Disgusting!' said the woman.

But Alec's gone, and what was imperfect between the father and the son will remain imperfect. All his life, Mark Rattigan will scourge himself with one screaming doubt: did the boy know, in those early years, that his father saw him as another man's child, unwanted? Perhaps Rattigan would never be able to answer that question. But she—Deborah—knew the answer:

"My daddy never wanted a little boy . . . he wishes I was dead . . . and so do I!" . . .

Up there in his room, now, waiting for the last grim act of his life's tragedy. They'd take him to the dead child, perhaps. It might be meaningful, to him, to touch the chill flesh he wasn't able to see. Deborah shuddered . . .

'You cold, love? It's the damp air, it's very deceiving. I've been in hot and cold flushes all day.'

It was the woman who spoke. There was a waiter hovering over them. He was looking at Deborah with brooding sympathy; he knew, of course.

'Join us in a drink, love.'

'No, thank you, I . . .'

'Oh, go on.'

In the end she accepted, out of cowardice. Then her private chrysalis was broken open, and she was bare for their probing inspection. No more brooding. Suddenly it was a blessed release to travel incognito along the humdrum path of everyday.

'Been here long, dear?'

'I came early Wednesday morning.'

'On your own, then?'

The waiter came back with a tray of tall glasses. He stooped and juggled with them, getting their orders mixed up. There was the splashing and padding of the running, barefoot children; shrill whoops of excitement. The ball landed plumb in the middle of the loaded tray. The woman screeched as the loaded glasses tumbled into her lap and shattered themselves round her feet.

'You bloomin' young hooligans!' The man leapt up, shaking his knotted fist. The children backed away, suddenly appalled. Then the oldest of them—the boy in the sweatshirt who had reminded Deborah of Alec—saw that avenging authority was nothing more than a little old man who spluttered. Moreover, he was wearing braces.

"Never let your braces dangle,
Never let your braces dangle.
Poor old sport
He got caught
And went right through the mangle!"

The others took up his piping treble, dancing in time; leaping up and down amongst the rainwater puddles, so that the overhead lights cast their thin, elongated shadows in the wetness. They danced and chanted, backing away when the man made a half-hearted rush towards them. And then they were gone, chanting still, into the darkness.

'Cheeky young devils! I'll have 'em!'

'Don't fuss yourself, love. It isn't worth it.' His wife was conciliatory. 'You'll only upset yourself.'

The mess was mopped and scraped up, and the good-humoured

waiter made light of the whole thing. Grunting and puffing, the old man let himself simmer down.

'Well, I 'spect you'd better bring the same again. Ours was whisky and orange. I forget what the young lady's was . . .'

They looked at Deborah.

'Why, what is it, dear? What's the matter with you?'

Deborah stared down at the wide puddles of water. The lights still wavered crazily on their ruffled surfaces, and she could still hear the children's voices coming from somewhere out in the darkness beyond the terrace. There was nothing else in the whole world but the dancing lights and the sound of the children.

That—and the blinding truth about the bird-man image!

'Are you taken ill, lass? Is there something we can get you?'

But she was brushing their hands aside, and edging past them. Running, pell-mell, along the terrace.

Halfway along the rhododendron-bordered road, she slowed to a stumbling halt, reaching for the low wall to support herself, sobbing breath into her aching lungs. She looked back at the blazing lights of the hotel, and they seemed very far away.

She should have gone straight to the two detectives in the hall: told them what she knew. They must have a car, or could borrow one.

Too late now, and too late to go back. She set off again, hand pressed over her thudding heart.

The round, white moon was perched on the tip of a craggy escarpment, and it cast long shadows down the glistening road. The moon is made of cream cheese; and I am going to die with horror at the thing I am running to see.

The dark heads of the rhododendrons flickered slowly past. Pray in time to your gusting breath: Our Father . . . which art . . . let me be wrong . . .

The bell-buoy's cracked clamour comes out of the grey mist, and the boat's blue sails rise and fall in the waves. Call Diana, but you'll never see her again; Diana's gone to join the bland-eyed boy who flamed down from out of the sky.

Call Icarus. He's not far away. Two horizons away, or less, the dark waves lap above his aluminium coffin. Call but he won't hear. Small fish swim in and out of his helmeted skull, and he never knew you.

Then the last, steep slope before the curve in the road, and the watchtower's eyeless window looking down on her. As she stumbled the last fifty yards, a wedge of black cloud slanted across the face of the moon, and everything was black.

She felt her way up the steps, fingering the worn edges of the stonework till she reached the door. The latch was sticky with wet rust, and would not move. She strained against it, two-handed; her cheek pressed against the woodwork, and the taste of her own tears in her mouth.

'Please, let it open . . . please!'

After an age, it yielded slightly, till she could curl her finger-tips round the edge of the door. Bearing with her whole weight, she was able to force the rain-swollen wood to grate slowly open. When there was enough space, she squirmed through, and felt the tongue of the latch rip the bodice of her dress.

It was dark in the chamber; only the dark grey rectangle of the small window.

Hands stretched out before her, she edged her way blindly forward, counting the shuffling steps with her heartbeats. The stone floor was wet underfoot.

Nine . . . ten . . . eleven and . . . her hands touched the far wall. With a small moan of despair, she leaned back against it and closed her eyes.

When she opened them again, a thick band of moon-light was

flooding in through the window, fighting the circular chamber with a blue-greyness; picking out the sagging timbers of the high ceiling; and revealing to her shocked eyes the small, thin form that lay stretched, face-down, near the middle of the floor.

'Alec!'

Then she was on her knees in the wetness, slipping her hands under the skinny body, nerves screaming at its coldness. She lifted the limp head and pillowed it against her, stroking the slime-covered cheek, rocking backwards and forwards on her haunches, an untaught keening-song breaking out of her throat.

Suddenly, she stiffened, and felt every hair on her body stand erect.

The thing in her arms had moved!

She stared down into the face: soiled-white in the gloom, sunken eyes closed, bloodless lips parted to show the uneven, childish teeth. And, as she watched and forgot to breathe, the lips quivered.

'Daddy . . .'

Her mind took up the whisper, and turned it into a great crescendo of sound. It soared through her consciousness and transcended it: a mighty paean of joy and life and love and deliverance. Laughing and crying, she kissed the tangled, wet hair. Scooping a hand under the bony knees, she picked him up, and he weighed nothing. Kissing him, still, she carried him over to the door, and strained it open till she was able to edge him through, feet-first. She trod carefully down the steps in the last of the moonlight; when she reached the bottom, the clouds had wiped out the moon again.

Across the bay, the lights of the hotel windows. In one of them sat Mark Rattigan, blind eyes searching the night; she willed the words to him, across the empty air: He's alive and safe, and he wants you, so nothing in the past will ever matter again . . .

A footfall in the darkness, near at hand: a stone crunching under a shoe.

'Who's there?' she called. 'Will you come and help me, please?' And when there was no reply: 'I'm over here, by the tower, and I've got an injured child with me.'

Silence. And then the footfalls began again, and they drew nearer. Slowly.

'Please answer me,' she heard her voice waver, and she fought to stifle a sudden, wayward unease. 'Where are you? I can't see you.'

The shape materialised out of the blackness, and resolved itself into the silhouetted figure of a man. He was hatless, and the jacket collar was pulled up to his ears, so the head was a grotesque dome rising straight from the shoulders. He walked with his hands held out before him, like a somnambulist, as he came slowly towards her, in silence.

'Who are you . . . *please*?' No use to hide her terror now; it was flaring up and consuming her will. He must sense it.

'Don't come any nearer!' she began to back away, clutching Alec more tightly to her.

He came on, matching her retreat, hands still extended towards her.

And then she saw the reason for the gesture; and the knowledge set her in screaming flight, still burdened with the unconscious child, along the rock-strewn path beyond the tower that led towards the sea—their only hope of escape, of living.

Stretched tautly between the hands was a length of rope—or a woman's stocking.

CHAPTER 13

When a rabbit evades the first snatch of the goshawk's scimitar talons in a vast, unconcealing meadow, she must run or die: no warm womb of burrow, no ditch's labyrinth; only space and movement for sanctuary.

The limp child was no burden when the path petered out and she had to stumble over broken rock and scrub. One half of her mind counted herself already dead; saving him was all that mattered to the rest. She lost a shoe, and kicked off the other. The soles of her feet were soon lacerated on the wet rock, and slippery with blood. She kept going.

The ground dipped, then rose again. Above her was the grey crest of a low hill, and beyond it might be anything: her numb mind grappled with the possibilities of a wooded copse for concealment; a road, with the friendly lights of cars; people sitting at the open doors of houses, calling to her with their warm, welcoming voices.

She stumbled to the crest, and heard the deep moan of the sea. A hundred feet below, the waves glowed with a million specks of green luminosity as they curled and surged about the pointed rocks. To the left, the ridge on which she was standing rose dramatically to a slab-sided peak; in the other direction it stretched towards the centre of the bay, and she could see the lights of the hotel beckoning her.

He was still behind her, hands held loosely by his sides now: domed head bent; plodding slowly up the slope, patient as the blinkered mules that toil round the creaking water wheels in the Maltese fields.

Sobbing, she went the only way that was left to her. Slowly, because the child's life was measureable, now, in time and distance. Unless the finger of God pointed down from the night sky and commanded a bridge to span the dark void of the bay, bis living would end where the ridge ended. Time was in the hands of their pursuer: the patient killer.

Fifty yards on, and now there was nothing but the sea to left and right. Ahead, the crawling waves of the bay, and the hotel on the far headland. The wind had died down; it was blowing in fitful gusts, and she could feel it touching both her ears when she faced the hotel. It brought her the sound of a three piece combo-guitar, piano and drums—labouring through the refrain of a McCartney-Lennon hit of yesteryear: Saturday night was party night, she'd been told. In the open space at the end of the bar they were jigging and swaying, heels clacking on the tiles: All My Loving.

Then distance had run out, and there was only time. She stopped at the end of the ridge and looked down at the black-fanged rocks beneath her feet. Then she was a priestess of a pagan cult, and the child in her arms was a precious life that only the gods could take for theirs, and she had only to let go; he would be caught in their eternal arms before his cartwheeling, thin body was pierced by the rocks—and carried away beyond the night clouds.

There was a bier-shaped, flat-topped rock near the edge. She lowered him gently, straightening the skinny legs, and folding the fingers together across his chest One kiss for each closed, long-lashed eye. To last for ever.

Blessedly, there was a loose piece of stone that yielded and came away at the first wrench. It felt rough and heavy in her hand: a weapon. She turned—and now the command of time was something she shared with the patient killer.

He had moved slowly too. Only halfway along the ridge, and coming at her with careful steps. And now the thread of death was held high above the faceless, domed head in a macabre gesture of exultation. Her skin crawled to hear the laughter of insanity.

Her back to the small life that she was fighting to protract, she moved forward to meet him, hefting the stone inexpertly. Ten paces from him, she prayed, and drew back her arm. The missile curved through the air and missed the domed head by a yard; the wild laughter soared to a cracked crescendo of mockery as the stone plummeted down into the breakers far below.

No retreat. It was as if she stood with her back to wall. When he moved past the spot where she was standing, she would be dead.

She closed her eyes and extended her hands, crooking her fingers to rake with her nails at the first touch of her killer.

Time passed, measured by the gusting of the wind and the slamming of the breakers—and nothing happened. She opened her eyes, and her heart lurched with sudden relief to see the ridge stretching, empty, before her. She whirled round—and screamed into the nameless face that was stooping as if to kiss the back of her neck: eyeless, mouthless, and unspeakably obscene.

She screamed till death closed about her throat and choked off her breath, forcing her eyes open so that she could not shut out the sight of the mouthless face that laughed down into hers.

Then even that was washed away from her open eyes by a great wall of grey water, and she was plunging down though the depths to where Diana was waiting, with sea kelp braided in the swaying fronds of her hair, and crab-mauled fingers reaching out to hold her for ever.

'Deborah . . . Deborah, it's all over . . . come to me . . .'

She resisted death: holding back from the embrace of those wavering, white arms; fighting to keep intact the slender thread that still bound her to the life of the upper air; to the realities of sunlight, the warm smell of babies' heads, rooks in high treetops, the sounds of a great city, leaves burning in Autumn, desire, gentleness, love . . .

Then the blank, grey wall was fading, and she was sucking in the night air through her slack lips. She was stretched out on the bare rocks, and they felt unbelievably soft and yielding under her nerveless body.

'You're safe, Miss Tarrant . . . safe!' Borg was kneeling beside her. The moon was out, and she could see his flecked eyes quite clearly.

'Alec?' she faltered.

'He's all right.' He nodded along the ridge. Then his head whipped round in the other direction. 'He's coming your way, Mike. Grab hold of him, man!'

The dome-headed grotesque was bounding along the spine of the ridge, away from them, slack arms flapping like the wings of a dying bird. It paused when its way was blocked by the bulky silhouette of another figure that had just scrambled up on to the ridge beyond.

'All right, Inspector . . . I've got him!' Agius's shout.

The killer turned, and Deborah had the sick thought that he was coming back to them. Instead, he broke into a run and—still running—gave a sudden, sideways swerve.

The running legs were still pounding empty air as he spun down into the darkness. From where she was standing—with her face pressed against Borg's hard shoulders—she clearly heard the flat, tearing sound of impact on the rocks below.

Her face was still hidden, and her shocked mind still reverberating with that last, awful sound, when Agius came up to them.

'See who he was, Mike?'

'Didn't get close enough to him.'

'I think he was wearing a stocking mask,' said Borg. 'Too dark to do anything now. We'll get a boat down there in the morning.'

CHAPTER 14

The good nuns masked their compassion behind brisk matter-of-factness. Sister Agatha had a spotless apron belted round her habit; and her hands were wrinkled-white from constant immersion in hot water. She stroked Alec's sleeping brow, smoothing back the damp forelock.

'Well, I think he'll be all right,' she said. 'And how long has he starved then?'

'Three days,' faltered Deborah. 'And three nights.'

'There was rainwater on the floor of the tower,' said Borg. 'That undoubtedly saved his life, Sister. And he had one good meal just before it happened: a big dinner of fish and chips before he was shut in the tower. That helped, too.'

'There is great resilience in the young,' said Sister Agatha. She smiled at Deborah, and the unaccommodating structure of her face was transformed to sudden loveliness. 'He was very near to leaving, but he will live now, thanks to God.'

When they quitted the dimly lit room, Borg took Mark Rattigan's arm, to guide him. Deborah looked back over her shoulder. Sister Agatha was taking her seat at one side of the bed. Young Detective-Constable Agius was already sitting opposite, a notebook resting on his knee, his gaze fixed on the face of the unconscious boy.

Borg drove them back to the hotel. As they swayed through the night, the scent of the newly washed earth came to them through the open windows, with the sound of the cicadas. Mdina was ahead, floodlit on its escarpment, gold and green.

It seemed to her that they were both—Rattigan and Borg—shouting soundless accusations of her guilt, and soon the silence would be ripped. She probed for the words to speak first—but they wouldn't come.

Borg spun the wheel, and the headlights played over a line of dry stone wall and a wayside shrine decked with dying flowers. 'We fell to rethinking the whole thing again tonight, Agius and I,' he said. 'It was the pattern of circumstances that had fooled us up to tonight, you see. The bodies of the two girls. They were both found in the sea, and we never thought to search anywhere else. While Harcourt was our man, the boathouse was the obvious place for him to have hidden Eileen Davis's body before dumping it into the sea under the cover of night. It was only when we shut our minds to Harcourt—in the face of the overwhelming circumstantial evidence against him—and accepted the possibility of a person unknown, that another hiding place near the beach was indicated. It followed, then, that we might find Alec's body in this hiding place. We acted on that, and the old tower—because of its sheer size and obtrusiveness—happened to be the first place we went to.' He half-turned his head and shot a glance at Deborah. 'We heard that wild laughter coming from the top of the ridge,' he said. 'And saw you struggling up there, against the skyline.'

She shuddered, as the words ruffled the surface of her own disquietening thoughts. Then she took a deep breath, clenched her hands very tightly, and said: 'It happened quite by chance, on the terrace. I saw some children playing among the rainwater puddles. A trick of the light cast their reflections on the water, elongating their legs, and making them appear tall and unearthly. I realised, then, what the image of the bird man might have been . . . that night.'

'Alec,' murmured Rattigan.

'He must have followed me to the tower,' she said. 'Perhaps he was concerned because I'd gone to look for the body he'd found there. And when I saw him staring up at the window, I saw his reflection, too. That was the image of the bird man, and I panicked. He came into the tower. He was there . . . near me, in the dark. And when I fled, I slammed the door behind me, jamming it tight . . .' she looked to each of them: Borg in profile at the wheel; Rattigan beside her, blind eves fixed ahead . . . 'and he couldn't get out. I shut him in that tower. For three days and three nights . . .

'I nearly killed him!'

At first light, they sighted the body from the top of the ridge, and marked the spot where the thing was bobbing, face-downwards, in the oily swell. Charlie Caesar was waiting for them on the beach, the unlit stub of a hand-rolled cigarette stuck in the corner of his grin.

'Hello, Joel. This is getting to be a regular thing. How's your cousin's baby getting along?'

'Fine,' said Borg. 'Let's go, Charlie.'

The postman held the bow of his boat while Borg and Bonnici paddled barefoot into the scummy shallows and climbed aboard. The engine started with the first turn of the crank, and they nosed in a slanting course across the bay towards the far headland. Borg was huddled with his elbow resting on the engine casing. In half an hour, the sun would be well up, and melting the tarmac in the streets of Valletta; right now, he thought, it was damned cold. He ducked when the seaward bow slapped against the oncoming wave, sending a splattering of fine spray into the boat.

And there was the tower. Sliding from sight, now, behind the jutting edge of the ridge that soared above them. Up there, near the edge, was where Deborah Tarrant had laid the boy down before she turned to face their attacker.

Deborah Tarrant . . .

'Whereabouts is it then?' said Charlie Caesar.

Bonnici pointed. 'Over there, about fifty yards farther along. See the two rocks sticking up together? It's lying between them.'

Charlie Caesar slackened the engine and swung the bow towards the base of the cliff. "I can't hold her there for long among the rocks,' he said. 'You'd both better go up front and make a snatch for it. Use the boathook.'

They could see it now: a limp puppet in a dark suit; one bloodless, white hand; the head was under water. Borg stood up with the boathook, steadying himself against the slow rolling, as the spent waves passed under them.

'If you miss first time, I'll back out and come in again,' said Charlie Caesar.

Ten yards. Five. One of the feet was bare; it was drained-white, like ivory.

'Now!' yelled Charlie Caesar.

Borg raked with the boathook, starting beyond the hunched shoulders. He felt a tug, as the hooked end caught in the collar of the coat. The engine rumbled astern, and the propeller wash creamed out from under the bows, frothing about the bobbing corpse.

They slid away from the rocks, bringing it with them.

Bonnici added his hands to the shaft of the boathook, and

together they drew their burden close alongside. It rolled over on the crest of a wavelet; and they could see the face, its features pressed flat and distorted under the stretched stocking.

'Mother of God, what a mess,' breathed Bonnici.

'The face is still all there,' grated Borg: and he reached down to grab the stocking foot that dangled like a scalp knot from the top of the head. The laddered nylon slid quite easily over the ashen features.

'Who is it, then?' said Bonnici. 'He's a stranger to me.'

'I know him,' said Borg. 'Interviewed him on Friday afternoon. Name of Richard Needham. Profession: school-teacher . . .' and because he had read all the reports and had a good memory for details, he added: 'home address: Stornaway Cottage, High Street, Woodbridge, Suffolk. Take us back now, Charlie.'

The high sun had sucked away every drop of moisture from the atmosphere; it was as if the previous night's rain had never been. Midges hovered above the sand-dusted sill of the open window, through which she could see the heat haze rising from the flat roofs of the houses opposite.

Agius came in with a tray of tea, and laid it on Borg's desk.

'I hope you're all sugar,' he said. 'I know the Inspector is. I've just come from the hospital, Mr Rattigan. Alec's fine, and sends his love.'

'They said we could visit him after lunch,' said Mark Rattigan.

Agius handed round the cups. He chuckled: 'He wouldn't let me leave, you know. Not after I told him I was in the Sirens. Next thing, I've got to teach him water polo. I told him next year. He wants to come back to Malta next year.'

Deborah looked down at her teacup, and kept her gaze focussed there till the door shut behind Agius. She looked up to see Borg regarding her thoughtfully; then the flecked eyes wavered back to the sheaf of paper on his desk.

'Where was I then?' he asked.

'You were saying that Alec's statement answered the last questions, and that the whole thing was now quite clear,' said Rattigan.

Borg nodded. 'I'll read it out to you,' he said, 'just as Agius took it down in shorthand at around three o'clock this morning, when the boy recovered consciousness . . .'

"It was on Tuesday morning, and Gloria was out in the speedboat with Danny. Kissing, I expect. So I went up to the tower, because it looked a good place to play knights. The door was hard to open. There was this dead lady lying there. I'd seen her on the beach, but I couldn't remember her name. I knew she was dead because she was very cold, but she didn't smell. She looked quite nice. Her watch was lying beside her, so I took care of it. She was going to be mine, you see.

"I didn't tell anybody, only Miss Tarrant, and she was very angry and said I must tell Gloria. This was on Wednesday. It was fish and chips for supper, and I ate down to the last chip but three before I showed Gloria the watch. She looked a bit funny, and said she recognised the watch, because she knew the lady who owned it. I don't think she believed me about the lady being dead in the tower, because she said she'd gone home to England, but Mr Needham would know.

"Gloria made me go to bed then. I asked her about the watch, and she said she'd ask Mr Needham for the lady's address in England. She said he was a dark horse all right.

"I went up to our room, but I didn't go to bed. When Gloria didn't come back after a while, I went up to the tower, to make sure that my lady was still all right. Miss Tarrant was there. I saw her go in the tower, and I went in after her. While I was feeling round for her, she rushed out and shut the door.

"I couldn't open the door. When it got light, I shouted for help, but nobody heard me. When I felt thirsty, I drank some of the water from the floor, and when I got tired I lay down. I did a lot of shouting.

"After that, I just slept . . ."

When he had finished reading, Borg laid the sheet of paper in the middle of his desk and very deliberately put a spun glass weight on top of it.

Dry-mouthed, Deborah stared at him. Rattigan shifted awkwardly in his chair, and said: 'So Gloria knew Eileen Davis. Well enough to recognise her watch and, presumably, to know that the name engraved on the back wasn't hers, but her mother's.'

Borg nodded. 'The mutual contact was Harcourt,' he said. 'I suppose Gloria knew he had his eye on Eileen. Being the sort of girl she was, she'd make it her business to know all there was to know about her prospective rival. Only, of course, even Harcourt couldn't keep two romances going at one time on the beach. The only real approach he made to Eileen Davis was at the casino on the Saturday evening. And I fancy he didn't get very far.'

'She'd already been propositioned by Needham!'

'I think so. We'll never know for sure, but I imagine Needham made his first overt move towards Eileen Davis about then. He knew she was due to go home on the Monday night plane. He'd been watching her, for sure, during the two previous weeks . . . inflaming his deranged mind . . .' When Deborah shuddered, his eyes flickered towards her . . . 'it's a nasty business, Miss Tarrant, and it doesn't get any better. Would you like to leave us?'

She shook her head.

'Well then,' said Borg after a pause. 'More guesswork. Gloria described Needham as a dark horse. That suggests to me that she'd seen him with the Davis girl. Alone. In compromising circumstances. Let's make it on the beach, on the Monday night. Needham meets Eileen Davis down on the empty beach on Monday night, after dinner. She's not greatly attracted to him, perhaps, but her holiday is just about over, and she's catching the plane in a few hours' time. Her luggage is already waiting in the hall, and she's paid her hotel bill. All she has to do is arrange for a taxi to take her to Luqa, or possibly Needham tells her he's fixed that already.

'There was a clear sky on Monday night, but the moon didn't rise till ten o'clock. She's sitting in the sand, leaning against one of Danny's beached sailboats. Needham comes down the steps from the hotel and walks towards her. His hands are in his pockets, and one of them is clenched round a nylon stocking . . . I'm sorry, Miss Tarrant.'

Deborah was on her feet and crossing over to the window. She looked out into the street and tried to control her trembling lips.

'Shall I go on?'

She nodded.

'He killed her with the stocking,' said Borg briskly. 'Gloria didn't witness the murder, of course, or she would have died sooner than she did. Perhaps she saw the Davis girl going down to the beach and decided she might be meeting Danny. Ho, ho! So she kept watch, and was amused to see the dark horse Needham slipping down to join her.'

'And afterwards, Needham carried her body to the tower,' said Rattigan. 'Why didn't he dump her in the sea and then—or just leave her lying where she was?'

'I think he planned to take the body well out to sea in one of the sailboats,' said Borg, 'so that it would be carried well away from the Maltese islands, and be lost out in the Mediterranean. But he couldn't do it then. Not on Monday night—with a cloudless sky, and a full moon due up at ten o'clock. Anyone looking out of their bedroom window would have seen the boat's white sail. But he had time to carry the body to the tower while it was still comparatively dark.'

'What about her cases?'

'He obviously dropped them in the nearest spot—over the headland at the end of the hotel terrace. They'd sink like stones. Our chaps are grappling for them right now.'

There was a long silence. Somewhere at the back of Deborah's sleep-starved mind was a thin gleam of consoling hope: something that stemmed from what Borg had been saying, but her mind could not encompass it. If only she could think clearly . . .

'Deborah.' It was Rattigan. She turned to face him. He was smiling towards her.

'Thank you for saving Alec's life,' he said simply.

'She certainly did that,' commented Borg. 'Twice!'

They were still talking, but it came to her through a euphoria of relief. The nightmare was over, now. The gyrations of the sick soul that had inhabited the body of the man named Richard Needham were ended. And Alec was blessedly safe.

'Gloria had a date with Harcourt after dinner on Wednesday night,' said Borg. 'In his room. A waitress saw her go in at about a quarter to eleven, and we've no reason to suppose that Harcourt lied when he said she left half an hour later.'

'Then she met Needham, and told him about Alec finding the watch,' said Rattigan. 'But where and when did she meet him?'

'We're in the area of speculation again, Mr Rattigan. But let's see what we have. Miss Tarrant went to the tower around about the time Gloria visited Harcourt, and Eileen Davis's body was no longer there.'

'It was the night of the storm,' said Rattigan. 'The sky was black with overcast. It was Needham's chance to take the body out to sea!'

Borg nodded. 'And the hotel was practically empty, with a large coach party gone to see the fireworks at St Julian's. That was the chance he'd been waiting for. No one to see him carry the body across the dark beach and take the boat out.'

'He could have done all that before twelve-fifteen, when Gloria came away from Harcourt's room.'

'Yes. It's likely that they actually met on the stairs, or in a bedroom corridor when Needham came back, soaked to the skin after his trip. Or she could have seen the light under his door. We don't know, and we'll never know, what her reactions were to Alec's story. She certainly couldn't have believed the bit about the body, or she would have raised a hue and cry. Maybe she was just wryly amused; just wanted to give the mild-mannered schoolmaster his girlfriend's watch for him to post back to her, to enjoy his embarrassment when he realised she must have seen them together on the beach at night.'

'And for that she died,' murmured Rattigan. 'She'd have mentioned Alec's pet body, of course. For the laughs.'

'He had to kill her,' said Borg. 'Needham made another trip out to sea that night. And when he came back, he went to silence the other person who could destroy him: a little boy who should have been sound asleep in bed . . .'

'But Alec was safely locked from harm. Thanks to Miss Tarrant!'

'Yes. God knows what he thought, but he must have been living on a knife edge from then on!'

* * *

They had an early lunch together in the C.I.D. canteen, and she ate just enough to please the manager, who had prepared her an omelette with his own hands. Borg was off duty, and insisted on driving them to the hospital to see Alec.

They crawled behind a farm cart, through an anonymous village dominated by a soaring basilica overlooking a shaded square. The narrow street into the square was crowded: veiled women in black, and men in Sunday best, little girls self-consciously lovely in minute wedding dresses, small boys in neat suits with white silk bows pinned to their lapels. The farm cart lurched to a halt, and its old driver turned with a wide-spread gesture of resignation and a gap-toothed grin.

Borg switched off the overheated engine. 'It's a First Communion,' he said, 'and they're all coming away from the church. We'll have to wait for a few minutes.' He lit a cigarette, and drew on it deeply. 'By the way, a message came in just before we left. Our chaps found Eileen Davis's cases in the water below the headland, where Needham dumped them on Monday night. There's a lot more, too: a Telex from Scotland Yard. They moved fast when we named the killer. The East Suffolk Constabulary knew Needham, all right. He's only recently escaped from being indicted on a serious charge—something concerning one of his girl pupils. It was dropped through lack of evidence, but there was enough to get Needham the sack!'

'He told me,' said Deborah slowly, 'he told me that he'd just been promoted.'

'They live in a make-believe world half the time, don't they?' said Borg. 'Schizophrenics. You feel sorry for them, in the sort of way you'd feel about a loathsome reptile that was sick and in pain. Poor devil.'

'Have his family been told?' asked Deborah. 'He came from a large family, and he gave me the impression that they were all very close to each other.'

'There's no family,' said Borg flatly. 'Needham was brought up in a succession of foster homes!'

Deborah looked away sharply, concentrating on the prim, self-absorbed faces of the passing children. They were all too shy to meet her glance.

'It could have been one of the unsolved disappearances of our time,' said Borg. 'The mystery of Eileen Davis, who checked out of a Maltese holiday hotel and was never seen again. That's the way he planned it, of course. But once he'd killed Gloria, the perfect crime was ruined. Enquiries would be started within hours—right there in the Sunshine Hotel!'

'He arranged to find Gloria's body himself,' said Rattigan. 'He must have had a reason for that.'

'Difficult to sort out the workings of a psychopathic mind,' said Borg. 'But there was a good and practical reason. For a man to rig a boat and sail it out to sea in the dark calls for a high degree of skill. Needham's performance—with the Milner girl as witness—was diabolically clever: an impersonation of a sailing tyro who only reached the grotto—where he'd dumped the body—because a favourable wind drove him there; and he had to be towed back. He was in a spot by Thursday morning, with Alec missing, but he went through with his plan to establish himself as a man who could never have handled the sailboat on a dark, stormy night. Found a girl to go with him as a witness . . .'

Borg's words broke through Deborah's absorbed contemplation of the passing children. 'He . . . he asked me first,' she whispered. 'He said he was hiring one of Danny's dinghies, and would I like to go along.'

'You'd have been safe on that occasion,' said Borg dryly. He switched on the engine. 'We're off again. And young Alec's waiting.'

There was a clear space through the centre of the village square. Some of the families lingered, gossiping, on the wide steps of the church, and on the pavements.

'You won't hold it against Malta, will you?' asked Borg gently. 'The things you've been through in the last few days—the horror and the suspense—none of these have any place here. What you see around you now is the real Malta.'

A dark-eyed child smiled shyly and fluttered a lace handkerchief. Deborah waved back to her till the small, white-gowned figure was out of sight.

CHAPTER 15

Their flight had just been called, but Alec was still up at the counter with his father, having led Rattigan by the hand to buy him one last orange squash.

Borg drained his lager, glancing out across the apron to the waiting plane. His mind returned to the last time they'd sat there together, the day they waited for Rattigan's plane. When he looked back at Deborah, her eyelids were downcast and she was toying with the strap of her handbag. They hadn't spoken since the others had left them.

'You'll soon be home,' he said.

'Yes,' she smiled without looking up.

Passengers were moving out towards the stairs, kissing goodbye, shaking hands. Someone moved up close behind him. He turned to grab a chair as it was overturned.

'I'm so sorry, Inspector! I just had to have a word with Miss Tarrant. One so seldom has chance on aeroplanes.' It was Mrs Marker, scarlet-faced under a flower petal hat. The Major was standing respectfully behind her, his poached-egg eyes wandering in embarrassment. Borg got up, recalling with relief how the Markers had returned to the hotel, that night, after it was all over, and he'd been able to dismiss the two officers who had been waiting to question the gallant major. 'What a very happy outcome, my dear,' boomed Mrs Marker. 'And so sensible of you to have stayed on for the rest of your holiday. We watched you many times on the beach, the Major and I. Quite the little family. And how heartening to see that little boy filling out again and getting some colour in his cheeks.' She tapped Deborah lightly on the wrist. 'But you'll have to watch him, my dear, as he grows older. He's delicate. Chest. He'll quickly outgrow his strength, I shouldn't wonder.'

Borg saw the pinkness touch the fine edges of Deborah's cheekbones, under her tan. Then she smiled into the woman's face. 'Thank you for pointing it out, Mrs Marker,' she said mildly. 'I'll write to Alec's father, now and then, and remind him of what you said.'

'Hem! Come along, m'dear. The aircraft's waiting. Good day to you, ma'am, and to you, Inspector.' Major Marker took his wife firmly by a muscular arm and led her away. The woman continued to stare indignantly over her shoulder at Deborah till she was out of sight.

'Nosey old bag!' murmured Deborah. And they both laughed.

'Are you going to marry Battigan?'

'He hasn't asked me,' she said soberly. 'And if he does . . . I don't know.' She picked up her handbag. 'We need each other, perhaps. Or we each need someone. Then there's Alec. I know I love him; I feel for him as I'd feel about my own child.'

He saw a movement out of the corner of his eye. Alec and Rattigan were crossing towards the stairs; Alec was holding his father's arm and waving to them.

Her hand slipped into his, cool and firm. 'Don't speculate about me, Joe,' she said. 'I'm Thursday's child, with a long way to go, and I'm a bigger and stronger person than the one who came to Malta. Now come and say goodbye to them.'

* * *

Five minutes later, he watched them emerge from the departure door beneath him, with the rest of the passengers for the London plane.

'Goodbye, Carmel! Goodbye, Loreto! See you again at Christmas, Papa!' The skyway between Luqa and Heathrow is a familiar path to the Maltese, and they make a big thing of seeing off their relations and friends. Flashing smiles and brown, upturned faces. The flurry of hands.

Alec was riding on his father's back, and Deborah was guiding Rattigan by the arm. She and the boy waved back at him till they reached the top step to the plane. Then Rattigan turned and raised his hand in valediction.

The fuselage doors slammed shut. A high whine of starters, and the four engines came alive in succession. The big aircraft lumbered away in a cloud of driven sand, and headed for the runway.

Borg didn't wait to see the take off. At the bottom of the stairs into the departure lounge, he had to pass a full-length painting of Our Lady of the Skyways. He flipped his cigarette into a waste bin, and made the Sign of the Cross.

ABOUT THE AUTHOR

Michael Butterworth was born in Nottingham in 1924 and served as a lieutenant in the Royal Navy during World War II. After the war, he studied and taught art for some years. He turned from drawing children's comic strips to writing scripts for them, quickly graduating to an editorship. Ten years later, he was an editor of women's magazines. Later, he became a full-time writer, which he did with a pet mongoose on his knee. He also had a hawk, peacocks, swans, a Newfoundland dog the size of a donkey, and many cats. He lived in Nottingham with his wife and six children. He passed away in 1986.

MICHAEL BUTTERWORTH

FROM OPEN ROAD MEDIA

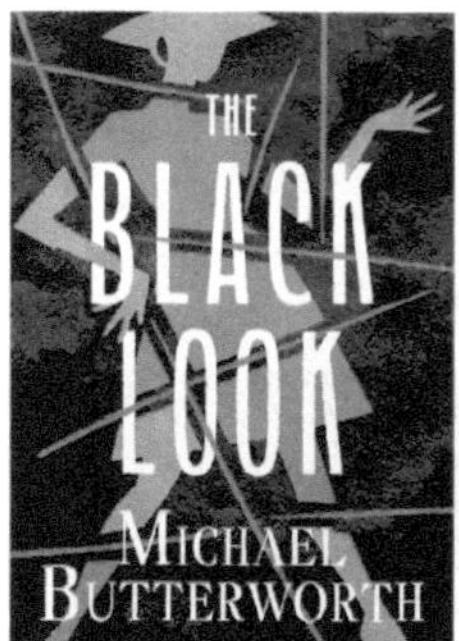

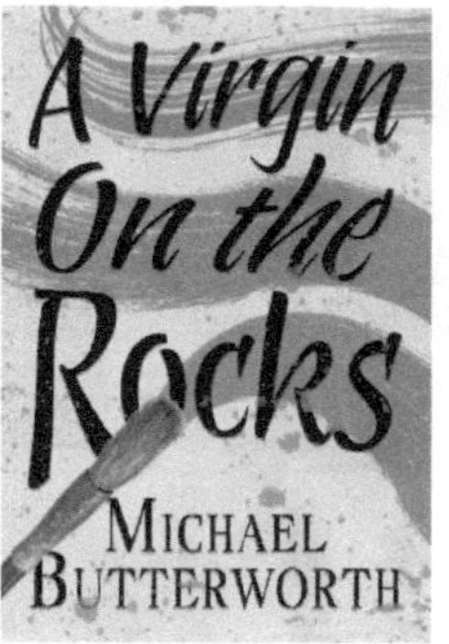

OPEN ROAD
INTEGRATED MEDIA

www.ingramcontent.com/pod-product-compliance
Lightning Source LLC
LaVergne TN
LVHW090608110826
845146LV00001B/301

* 9 7 9 8 3 3 7 2 0 4 3 5 2 *